RESISTANCE

Josephine Boyce

First published in 2017 by Josephine Boyce

For you rebels. Keep fighting.

The Battle for Carreo

Worlds fall around us
Blood, ashes and tears
Lives vanish before us
Oh the years, the years, the years!

We fight with fist and metal
With heart, with body, with mind
We bite, rip, claw our way through
Blind, blind, blind

And we RAGE RAGE RAGE
Until the mountains come down
And we rage rage rage
Until the mountains come down.

Cyrus Oberon, Auria, 1902

RAGE

Her breath hangs in the air momentarily before dissipating. She doesn't move. There's a tickling of a breeze — she makes the smallest of adjustments.

She waits. She's good at waiting.

There's a hum inside her head; she squeezes her eyes shut to will it away. She opens them, and her moment comes.

She compresses the trigger without hesitation, without remorse. Her target goes down.

Her audio 'com pings a message — *"Report back to base."*

She complies.

She always complies.

WEEK TWENTY

CASSIA

The Global Defence Organisation is finally falling in Auria, but there are many battles still to be fought to defeat it.

The ground is melted and there is ash beneath my boots. The air, still hot and laced with smoke, stings my lungs. Ahead, beneath the haze from the dying furnace of flames, a town begins to fall in on itself, collapsing after the burning destruction of the GDO. I stop, coughing. We were too late.

I didn't understand who our enemy was before, not really, then I watched cities burn because of them, and I began to see everything more clearly.

The air is scorching my eyes, and I have to hold my sleeve over my nose and mouth to limit smoke inhalation.

"We need to get clear of this smoke." Dune waves us to the east, away from the drifting dust of carnage.

We are a small company; it is easier to manoeuvre in small groups and we've kept our name from the night of the prison break — Sault. Dune, our leader and senior member of the Resistance, Echo, his second in command, Ian, the unassuming assassin, Ham, a Resistance fighter, Drummer, Jono, Shreya, Yve, Luca and me, all of us ex-GDO soldiers, all of us traitors to the regime. We turn as one and head away from the thick cloud, the crackle and crumble of the devastation falling in harmony with our crunching footsteps as we leave the molten tarmac. When we're in cleaner air Dune stops, and we group around him.

"We need to check for survivors." He brings up a map of the area on his tablet. We're just over the border of Old France, and he shows where we'll approach, making sure that the wind is at our backs so that we don't suffer from inhaling too much smoke. "There isn't any backup. The nearest unit to us is half a day out. There may be hostiles."

He doesn't ask if we're okay with it, if going into expected danger is something we want to opt out of — we're his soldiers, we follow orders. Besides, this is why we're here — to help people, to save people from the GDO.

The fire couldn't have started that recently as the flames have nearly died down almost to nothing, but the heat remains, and the smoke. Our faces are smudged with grey as we walk as silently as we can, as a unit, through the streets. I can't see how anyone could survive this. As we near the central streets we start to see bodies, although it's hard to see who they once were. Their bodies are blackened from burns, red with blood. My eyes water from smoke and tears. I see the same in every member of our team. The corpses increase the closer to the centre of the town we get. We stop outside a square and Dune motions for us to take cover. I squat down in the charred remains of a doorway that barely blocks me from view. A few metres away, a body lies curled in on itself. I look away.

Before us we can see GDO soldiers, their faces covered with masks, digging up the two lawns that lie either side of a fountain. To their right is a pile of bodies, heaped together as though they aren't people. Tears fall silently down my face, making tracks through the soot glued to my skin. My hands are shaking and my vision is slightly blurred. I am about to faint. I take slow, deep breaths through my sleeve and then I feel a hand rest gently on my shoulder. I turn to see Ham, looking as pained as I feel. His comfort clears my head because before me is a seasoned soldier and he feels it too. We have a mission to complete.

Dune signals for us to fan out as much as possible. I stick with Ham as we make our way further east, and we crouch down behind a burnt-out car. Our earpieces are in. We just have to wait for the signal. Ham is slightly in front of me, his gun raised. I notice we're breathing in unison. Dune gives the signal and Ham opens fire. Two soldiers in

Ham's sight line fall as I cover him. He reloads and I step forward. I'm unable to steady my hands, but as I start to pull the trigger, the last soldier falls; I notice the shot came from Echo. I'm relieved that I was saved from having to take action.

We make our way forward, me covering Ham's back again, waiting for any movement. None comes. I continue to stay on watch as some of the others check the bodies. A few shots are fired; one soldier must have survived their initial wounds. I try to focus on my role, but my eyes keep drifting to the pile of bodies they were about to inter in a rudimentary mass grave. I taste bile and swallow it down. I feel a panic so intense that all I want to do is run away from this atrocity. But I stand firm, my eyes scanning for movement.

Dune sends out Yve, Echo, Drummer, and Ham to search the surrounding area. When they return they report that there are no more soldiers to be found, and so with our hands gloved we begin to carefully lay out the bodies that have been discarded so abysmally. Luca and I work together to carry a single person at a time and lay them out, putting them at rest as best we can. Jono and Shreya have been tasked with finding as many sheets as they can, and when they come back they begin to blanket the dead, giving them a shroud to show them as an individual deserving of their passage into death.

We search the street for hours. Anyone who survived the fire we find with either their throats cut or their bodies punctured with bullets. The GDO were gruesomely thorough. I don't stop to wonder what this town did to deserve this; usually there isn't much of a reason.

As the sun starts to set, we slowly make our way back out of the town as another team of Resistance fighters comes to take over from our dark task before the Red Cross arrives. They slap us each on the shoulder as they pass, not saying a word. No words need be said at times like these because we all feel the same thing: anger, devastation, abhorrence.

As we walk away from the horrors we've seen, I begin to think about the medallion my dad had kept — the one I had used as inspiration for the message I sent to help free him from prison — "Whatever rightly done, however humble, is noble." But what if something is done for the right reasons but causes death and destruction beyond imagining? Is it still noble then? I can't seem to reconcile nobility with the death of thousands, the deaths that I helped cause as the linchpin to the rebellion that has now swept across our continent. Was that town annihilated because of what I started? Luca tries to tell me that I'm being arrogant and melodramatic taking all the "linchpin" credit, but I know he's trying to ease my burden, because despite all that's happened and all that has been said, he's still trying to protect me, even if that means protecting me from myself.

"Poo break!" We all turn to Ham in surprise. "What? I need a crap."

We're all shocked into laughing. Although Ham is new to our number, he was in Dune's regiment before the GDO took over, and he already feels like part of our team.

"I'm so jealous," moans Jono. "I haven't been able to evacuate my bowels in days thanks to these military rations."

"Who says evacuate bowels?" Luca asks, bemused.

"Professionals," Jono responds primly.

"Professionals?" Yve gives Jono a confused look.

"Doctors and the like." We roll our eyes at him, then Drummer goes on to offer some unhelpful advice involving a twig, which makes us all groan in revulsion.

We have spent the past two weeks together in Vayo, planning as well as resting, although Luca's leg is still giving him trouble after he was shot when we tried to escape GDO capture, but he refuses to slow us down. I know walking is still causing him a lot of pain. We only had one day in a truck, and I'm sure he misses the luxury of resting his leg. His bravado irritates me a little — can't he just admit to the pain? It's not as though anyone would think less of him, but he insists on carrying on, being there when the GDO fall.

It was hard to leave Vayo, knowing that we were going from relative safety into a war. My parents tried to stop me, but I still left. It was difficult to do, considering I'd risked everything to help my dad and the other political prisoners escape from jail, to leave my mum when she was only just starting to recover from her illness. I don't really understand what drove me to go, how I had any strength left to leave, but I need to continue this fight; there's an urgency to it that I can't shake. It helps having Luca by my side.

I just hope that the remaining Resistance in Vayo will keep our families safe. Keep Emma safe, the last surviving member of Jake's family.

We wait patiently for Ham to finish, knowing that his comedic timing wasn't accidental; he knew we needed to be distracted from our thoughts of the horror around us. Usually Drummer or Jono are the ones to take the helm on lightening the mood, but not today. Ian lies on his back cleaning his glasses, his rotund middle rising and falling hypnotically. I asked him the other night how an accountant becomes an assassin, and he replied, "I think you'll find that most accountants have murderous tendencies." I'll definitely be a lot more wary around accountants in future.

Shreya isn't really talking to me; I think she feels betrayed because we didn't tell her we opposed the GDO back when we were all based in Camburg. That, and because I'm with Luca and she isn't. I feel bad about how we treated her and I'm possibly over-compensating for my guilt by offering her pieces of my rations and cleaning out her canteen. She seems pretty comfortable accepting my offers, though. Yve's wildness has dimmed since Jake's death; loss takes pieces of you, but I hope it's a piece she can get back, because her spirit is so vibrant it draws you in and makes the fight seem worth all the risks.

Dune and Echo are constant in their leadership. Although Dune is our leader, he often defers to Echo for decisions because of her past experiences as a spy inside the top ranks of the GDO army. It's good to have them in charge and not have to come up with strategies ourselves. Looking back, I realise how naïve I was instigating a jail break, but I suppose without that naivety I would never have taken such risks and my father would still be in prison and my parents separated. The GDO would have complete control of Auria, my home country, by now. Instead, they're scrambling to maintain control.

Dune scrolls through his data pad — we were each given one before we set off on our journey and it's nice to feel connected again — and scans the horizon.

"We need to take a different route, GDO soldiers have been spotted two miles away." Dune tucks away his tablet and stands as Ham returns, and we head out.

As we walk, I try not to think about Simon and his betrayal of our plan to the GDO, but fail. I don't hate him for what he did — we were successful after all — but I'm not sure I can forgive him for his weakness. Maybe that's my own weakness. Maybe now we're working with seasoned professionals we won't encounter similar issues — they don't have to come up with strategies in a shower room, like we did in Camburg, for a start.

Before we left, Dune had briefed us on the Resistance plan to destroy the GDO: we need to weaken their hold on Old Europe by interfering with their propaganda, intercepting weapons deliveries, and destroying revenue streams. Without propaganda to strengthen their position, more people will join the Resistance, bringing weapons to arm its growing numbers. And without money, the GDO's power has no foundation for its control. When their position is teetering, the Resistance will enter Utonia and topple the regime.

Sounds easy, but as Ham said, "No battle plan survives contact with the enemy." It sounded impressive, but it turns out some guy called Helmuth von Molke said it first. We're relying on old intel, dispersed numbers, and recently the GDO have been revealing some impressively frightening new technology. They haven't been idle whilst occupying our lands, that's for sure.

That night we make camp in an abandoned church, which reminds me of my first days as a recruit for the GDO. I go to sleep with Luca curled around me protectively, hoping that tonight he'll be able to keep the demons that torment my sleep at bay.

But they still come.

KOHLER

Major Jay Kohler was standing in his room as he slowly began to button his shirt, remembering the moment he had pushed himself up from the floor at the scene of Cassia Fortis' execution and had looked around to see there were many dead, including Major Burgin. He smiled at the memory.

He'd barked orders as his head throbbed from a blow, calling for some of the remaining soldiers to check the wounded and for others to pursue the escaped prisoners. He had wanted that little bitch alive — she'd tried to ruin his reputation and he wasn't even allowed the satisfaction of carrying out her execution himself. At the time he'd thought it was better she'd got away; he'd always enjoyed the chase. But they hadn't caught her — not yet, anyway.

In his room, Kohler examined his face — there wouldn't be any permanent scarring from the scratches Fortis had given him; they were barely visible now. He touched his cheek with relish. He had enjoyed their fight, how she had bucked like a frightened little antelope, and him, the lion. Yes, he enjoyed that memory a lot.

There was a knock on his door.

"Yes?" he called, annoyed at the timing of the interruption; he had been about to revel in his memory.

"Phone call for you, sir." Kohler flicked his tongue against his teeth in annoyance, but he slipped on his trousers and went to take the call.

He grabbed the phone off the waiting soldier. "Kohler." He knew the voice on the line well — it was the general who had promoted him to take over from Major Burgin. Kohler smiled into the phone; clearly he had proven himself in his new position and was finally being relocated.

"Remember your duty. Peace and prosperity."

"Peace and prosperity," Kohler said handing the phone back to the waiting soldier. He made his way to his office and sat behind the large desk, taking it in for the last time. Leaning back, he realised that all he had been through, all he had done, had been worth it to get to where he was. His goal was close. But first, the little bitch was going to have to pay.

RAGE

As she makes her way back to base, a five-mile trek across desecrated land, she listens for the moment when she'll no longer be drowning in herself. There, a whisper — no, a mumble. It wasn't enough. As she walks, her mind tumbles and she begins to run, to get back to headquarters, to get out of her head. Being alone, truly alone, is the only thing that frightens her now. They had done everything they could possibly think of to break her, but they never actually succeeded, because they didn't know that they had given her the only thing she needed. They had made it so that she was never, ever alone.

Sometimes, though, when his shifts conflict with hers, she can feel the tick and itch of her nightmares crawling up to the surface.

She runs faster.

CASSIA

Luca kisses my temple to wake me; I feel as if I've only just fallen asleep. The world burned in my dreams and I'm becoming afraid that my nightmares might slip through the cracks into my waking hours. Drummer's whistling when I finally manage to sit up, and Jono is overtly flirting with Shreya and Yve, simultaneously. They appear to be humouring him more than anything. I go and sit with Ian; it's comforting to be near our most lethal assassin sometimes. Ham, Dune, and Echo are having a serious discussion, half hidden by the pulpit. I watch Ian sharpen his knife, the one I've seen slide into flesh.

Luca sits down next to me, drawing me from my mental downward spiral. I need to stay focused; I can feel myself slipping away into a world of muted sounds and hazy edges. Luca hands me my rations, and I manage a smile for him and lean into his shoulder. I still can't face being too intimate with him after what Kohler tried to do to me when we were stationed in Camburg, but I'm lucky I have Luca because I doubt many people would be as understanding and patient as he is. We finish our breakfast in silence.

"We should reach the others today, let's load up." Dune bends down and picks up his pack. There's an impatient energy surrounding him. He's eager to be back with his unit, to be back in the thick of it. Rescuing us in Auria was a necessary diversion from his original plan. He knew that if he helped us he could also fire up the rebellion by hitting back at the GDO when we took down their internal network, effectively making them blind to our actions. The Resistance took that opportunity and staged multiple attacks that night, but Dune coming to Auria separated him from his men, from vital intel and supplies. I can tell he needs to be leading from the front physically as well as figuratively.

My data pad pings with a message from Clive, still bunking down in his basement in Auria's capital, Amphora, and helping us where he can.

"We need to change course, there's a convoy of GDO vehicles on the northern route," I say, turning the screen so Dune can have a look.

"Let's move out."

I let the happy bantering of my companions slide into the background as I wonder about my choices. I want to fight the GDO, and I want to stand up for what is right, but the more I think about it the more I wonder if this is the right way to go about it. I jumped at the chance to be doing something, but maybe I should have taken the time to really consider my options. They're doubts I don't feel I can share, they're doubts that I worry Luca would consider unfounded, and I don't want to lose his respect or his trust. Everyone here needs to believe that I am 100% in; any hesitation is a danger, a liability, to the group. I want their trust. I need it; it's what keeps me going, the camaraderie. We are brothers and sisters in arms, and without them, I don't believe that I could so much as get up in the morning, let alone fight an oppressor.

I force myself out of my own head and try again to improve the frosty relationship I have with Shreya.

"So, do you know where Pranav is?" I ask tentatively, annoyed with myself that I didn't think to offer to have him join us when we left Auria.

"He's already with Dune's group in Old France." From her expression, I can tell she's irritated I've only just asked after him.

"He is?"

She turns to me, her beautiful big brown eyes blazing with anger. "We always intended to oppose the GDO, my joining up was part of my test. You'd have known this if you'd trusted me enough to let me in on your plan instead of using me."

Her words sting and I don't blame her for how she feels, but honestly, we're at war, how is anyone to know who to trust when you're inside the enemy camp. Also, it just pisses me off — it's good to be feeling anger, to feel anything.

"You know what? Forget it. We weren't to know which side you'd be on, stop taking it out on me. You're here now."

She turns away from me and I fall back and re-join Luca and Ham. Ham's telling another of his old army stories; Luca is only half listening, aware of what I'd just said, and I can see he doesn't approve, that if I weren't some damaged thing he'd berate me for being unfair. But I am damaged — by the loss of my best friend Jake, by Kohler's assault — so instead, as he listens, he reaches out and holds my hand loosely. It's these small actions, the smallest things he does, that show he's always aware of me. This is my lifeline, and I take it, even though I know in this moment that I don't deserve it. I was cruel, but it felt good to be something other than numb.

Our detour means we have to spend another night on the road, an extra precaution until we're in a safer location. As we lie in an abandoned barn, I hear Yve's uneven breathing. I can taste her hidden sorrow at the loss of her boyfriend. I crawl over to her and hold her hand, rest my forehead against hers.

"Sometimes," she whispers to me, "It just takes me by surprise and hits me again, that he's not here."

I have to swallow hard so that I can speak; my throat feels closed up. "Remember how he used to do stupid accents?"

She lets out a quiet laugh. "He was really bad at Northern Irish."

"But always insisted on doing it." I find a smile in my sadness, at the memory of him, how he was. He was always so full of life, and it still doesn't feel real that all that vivacity was gone. We lie there quietly until I feel brave enough to finally confess, "I'm sorry I didn't save him."

"Me too." Both our hands are clasped together now as we lie face-to-face on the cold floor. There's so much more I want to say, and I can see in Yve's eyes that she feels the same, but somehow, as we lie there, cocooned together in sorrow, no more words need to be spoken.

There, in the quiet, we mourn Jake. We lay him to rest and we acknowledge our grief. We are broken but we will heal. After all, we have each other and we have our friends. We will ride these waves of loss together.

RAGE

She's out of breath and sweating when she reaches the base, her short black hair sticking to her face. They won't let her grow it or cut it shorter; they say it will make her look like an innocent child in case she's ever captured, even though she is just an innocent child. At least, she thinks, the run was good exercise — she is all too aware that she needs to keep her fitness up. She tucks her too damn short hair behind her ears, wishing she could just shave it all off, to feel the soft breeze gliding over her skull, soothing the buzzing in her brain.

Her 'com sends an alert; she's to report in for a briefing. She's annoyed she hasn't had anything to eat yet, and she doesn't want to go out on another assignment straight away. She wants to see him, she wants to stop the whirring in her head that won't go away won't go away won't go away.

He needs to wake up; she needs to wake him up.

She walks into the briefing room, still a little out of breath and red-faced. The room is filled with people working at computers, despite the fact it's only just gone 6 a.m. At one end of the space is a large white table with a computer screen built into it. They have a satellite image of a map already loaded onto the screen. The general is standing straight-backed with his legs shoulder-width apart; he's tall, broad shouldered, and has cold eyes, eyes she always makes herself look into. She won't let them taste her fear, not any more. She finds him ugly, although she supposes there are uglier people, but there is something innately hideous about him. He doesn't brief her; her captain does. He's sort of on the skinny side for a solider, his eyes slightly bulging, his nose a little bit hooked, with dark hair and a widow's peak. He doesn't look like a GDO soldier you would fear, but she knows what he's capable of — she knows it all too well.

"We've located a Resistance cell and we want you to infiltrate it," the Captain says.

"Yes, sir."

"You'll be dropped in tonight, wait until morning. Set a charge here." He zooms in on the map and points at a petrol station, no doubt one that is now abandoned. "You're close enough to their base that they'll come and check on it. Stay within enough range of the blast to get singed; you need injuries if they're to take you in." He hands her some earplugs. "Wear these, as we'll need your hearing intact if you're going to spy, but don't forget to feign temporary deafness."

"Yes, sir." She refrained from rolling her eyes; she's been briefed on countless scenarios like this hundreds of times.

"And remember; don't give them any clues about the tech you carry."

"Yes, sir."

"Get whatever information you can. We need to know where other Resistance units are based, how wide its network really is."

"Yes, sir."

He turns to the general. "Far too many of them mutter to themselves when they're responding to links or touching the implant. It takes up too much of our time to break the habit." He sighs as though he has far too many problems, that this one is just a trifle in an extensive list. "You've been with us long enough, Rage. I expect you to be invisible to them — just some unlucky orphan kid that was in the wrong place at the wrong time when the GDO stopped by. Got it?"

"Yes, sir." Sometimes she finds it odd that they don't see her as a kid anymore. She is a soldier, that much is true, but she is still only twelve, or is it thirteen? That's a kid, still, right? She doesn't know why she is bothered — she'd much rather be seen as a soldier than a child — but, still, it is her first undercover operation, and it would be nice to be treated like some of the other more useless recruits by being pandered to a little. But, then again, if they are still soothing you they are also still beating you, so maybe she should stop bitching about being sent out undercover alone, and get on with the job. She just hopes the Resistance fighters had decent food.

Knight has a room to himself; the others don't like to share a room with him because of his night terrors. When you have to get up early for duties or drills, you don't want to be kept up because one of your bunkmates is screaming. So Knight's room is an old cupboard that they've managed to squeeze a metal camp bed into. The mattress is thin and stripy and shows through the scratchy white sheets, but she knows Knight likes it in the old store room — he has his own little window, a shelf for his collection of leaves, twigs, and stones, and it smells clean, unlike the dorm room which generally smells of a mixture of stale and fresh urine because so many of the boys still have accidents, but no one says anything; you'd get a beating if you did and so they just let the pee soak into their mattresses. She has heard Knight thinking that he's relieved he managed to get control over that one small thing.

Rage opens the door to Knight's room and shakes him awake.

"Go away, Rae."

"Wake uppp."

"No, I don't have to be up yet."

"I'm going away for a while, this is the last time I'll see you for a few days."

Knight opens his big dark eyes, his silky black hair falling over his cheek — longer than regulation, but they don't bother him with things like that anymore. He puts his hand to her cheek and looks pained.

"It won't be for long," Rage thinks.

"You don't know that," Knight replies in her mind, his lips never moving.

"'Course I do. I'm just infiltrating a camp; I'll be out before you know it."

"A Resistance camp?" Knight's eyes light up.

Rage looks around, panicked.

"Will you stop freaking out? You know that our Symbio link is protected," Knight reassures her.

"I know, but you can never be too careful." Rage shoves her hands into her pockets and hunches her shoulders.

"I am very careful and there's no way they're breaking the encryption I added."

"I know, I know." Rage lies down on the bed next to Knight and looks up at the cracked ceiling.

"How was your mission this morning?" Knight turned onto his side to face her.

"A success."

Despite her face remaining expressionless, and her response being perfunctory, Knight can hear what was unsaid. *"Will you come down to the 'coms room today and stay with me until you go?"* He turns to her, his face betraying more than he could ever physically say.

"Every minute until I have to leave."

Knight closes his eyes and lets out a relieved sigh.

Rage blinks rapidly, her eyes suddenly stinging but the buzzing in her head gone. She slides her shoulder under his and closes her eyes, catching as much sleep as she can before Knight's shift begins.

CASSIA

We finally reach the camp, but it's not at all how I'd imagined. It's at the top of a hill in the midst of fields and trees; it's picturesque, which seems out of place, considering the war we're fighting. The building is a large old farmhouse with sprawling outhouses, possibly even once considered a chateau, but its grandeur has faded over time. The position is perfect, elevated to give a clear sight line all around, isolated so that locals don't spy or interfere, and big enough to store weapons, vehicles, and Resistance fighters.

We trudge up the steep path, feeling our tiredness more now that we're so close to our destination. All I can think about is having a proper shower and putting on some clean clothes — we've had to stay in our army kits in case we encountered a GDO patrol, so they've really started to stink.

"Looks like there'll be enough privacy, so you'll finally be able to drum away again, bud." Jono elbows Drummer.

"Is that all you can think about?" Drummer asks his best friend.

"Of course it is. What's wrong with you?" Jono seems genuinely upset.

"It's just, you sat in a turd yesterday, thought you'd want a shower first. I *hope* you wanted a shower first." Laughing, Drummer keeps a safe distance from Jono, who definitely smells worse than all of us put together.

My laugh sounds far away, like it's coming from someone else. There is a whole other part of me now, the one that reacts in the way that's expected. The rest of me is kept apart, safe, deep inside where nothing can reach me.

As we get closer I notice that the shutters, which appear brown, were once painted sky blue but the paint has peeled over time. We pass two sentries that I can see as we make our approach, and when we reach the front door of the farmhouse it's flung open by a man who beams when he sees Shreya. Pranav runs to his sister and picks her up, laughing with relief. He goes around the group shaking our hands but salutes Dune. I don't recognise Pranav from Auria's GDO recruits; he enlisted with Shreya before we did, and so our paths have never crossed. He's not much taller than her. His dark hair is and longer than army regulation would allow, and he has a smile so disarming that I hope I'll be able to get along with at least one of the siblings.

The inside of the farmhouse is polished oak that's scuffed and worn, wallpaper curling in the corners, and paint that's faded and flaking. Despite its tired state, it feels as if it was once a home, that it was loved. That feeling permeates each wall and creaking floorboard, and I finally find some form of comfort in this dusty, slightly broken piece of the past.

We're taken through the centre of the house and out the back door, which leads to the outbuildings. One, a two-story barn, has been set up as a barracks. Camp beds are neatly lined against opposite walls that run the length of the space on both floors. The pool house is our bathroom and shower room; fortunately, there are two bathrooms, even though it's nowhere near enough for the number of soldiers, which I estimate to be around forty in our building alone. The pool house also doubles as our mess; sofas are clustered together to make as much seating as possible — floral sofas, ripped leather ones, others with stained fabric, and a couple of antique-looking dining chairs that I'm pretty sure would have cost a lot of money before the war. There isn't any value in such things now.

We're told to wash and then go to the main house for a briefing. Drummer offers to shower with Jono to "save time", and Jono responds by stripping off all his clothes and running naked to the mess, calling Drummer to follow him. Drummer laughs and grabs Jono's towel and makes his way to shower by himself. Ham bellows with laughter. "I haven't had squaddies with such good value for ages."

"You can keep them in your room if you like, they *never* sleep," Yve offers.

"I'll let you lot enjoy their company. I'm all for some privacy." Luca gives me a meaningful look, which makes Yve roll her eyes. We've not had any privacy since we got together in Camburg, always sharing a room with the rest of Sault squad, although we did manage to find ways to be together. It's a shame the six of us — the lower ranking members of Sault squad — will have to share the top floor with a few others we are yet to meet.

As always, showering after days spent without one was the best feeling in the world — I almost, almost felt like myself again. There is still a hollowness inside, that dark place that feels like a bruise on my soul. But Luca is with me in the now-empty dorm, and he's clean, which makes a big difference to the hug he gives me. He kisses the top of my head and tells me he almost took Jono up on his offer, seeing as I didn't make any advances. I laugh, a real laugh, and then kiss Luca properly for the first time in days, and as I do, a little of that fogginess lifts, the bruise turns from black to dark purple. But as I feel him responding to me, I pull away, everything inside me slamming shut.

"I'm sorry." I look down, not able to face him, too ashamed.

"However long it takes, you know that."

"I'm not being fair, it's not like… you know… nothing really happened." Because Kohler never got the chance, I fought him off; it doesn't make sense for me to feel this vulnerable.

"Yes it did, you don't have to play it down to me, and I know it's not just that, I know that it all weighs on you." He takes my hand in his and I dare to look at him. His expression is so open and caring, and yet I feel irrationally annoyed at him. I almost want him to push me, to force me out of whatever is happening. I want to scream and yell and at the same time, I want to hide and cry. I'm a disaster.

"Luc, you know you don't have to wait for me. With everything that's going on—"

"Stop." He holds up his hand and looks offended. "This is the only time I'm letting you get that far into pushing me away. You're not going to push me away because things are hard. You got it? We're in this together, no matter what. You take all the time you need. For once, within the army, we have private shower cubicles, I can hold out." He gives me a gentle smile. "I will wait for you, Cassia Fortis."

"You're so revoltingly cheesy." But despite this, I can't hold back a smile.

"It's why you love me." He straightens his collar with an arrogant flair.

"No, it's not, but I do love you, even though I don't know how to show it right now." I tighten my ponytail and wonder where the girl who had felt complete calm at her own execution had gone.

"I know, baby bear." He elbows me gently.

"*Baby bear?!* Urgh! What was that?" I grimace at him.

"No? I thought it was time we tried nicknames."

"No, we're not doing nicknames."

"Why not?" He looks put out, but I know that he's just trying to wake the old me up.

Without saying anything, we begin to make our way to the farmhouse. "Because nicknames make me cringe."

"But, bubba!" He grins as he says it, making me laugh.

"Luc, I swear, if we're not careful one will stick."

Drummer runs up to join us. "What will stick?"

"Trying to think of pet names," Luca says, matter-of-factly.

"Don't say pet, it makes me feel like a puppy or a sidekick — and I am no one's sidekick."

"I don't think anyone would ever think of you as a sidekick, Cass." Drummer smiles at me. "You're far too good at creating uprisings."

"That's true — remember when you started that campaign at school to have puddings returned to the cafeteria?" Luca asked.

"It was criminal! They couldn't take away our cake!" I feel my old indignation returning at what felt like the crime of the century. Back then, things were an awful lot simpler.

"Bet she got them to bring pudding back," Drummer says with conviction, as we make our way into the hall.

"Of course she did, with *custard,*" Luca says with considerable flair.

Drummer's eyes go wide with appreciation. "Well! Custard! See, never a sidekick. Maybe you should call her pudding pie." Drummer grins at me as we stroll into the briefing room and take seats next to Shreya, and, I might be imagining it, but it looked like he blushed a little when he made eye contact with Pranav. Echo strolls in — her hair is redder than before, her lips perfectly painted. All eyes follow her in; it's impossible not to stare at her. She takes a seat at the front, and then Dune walks in. He stands in front of the room full of soldiers. Looking around, I'm assuming this space used to be a large dining room — our chairs are old kitchen ones, wooden wine crates, empty gun and ammo boxes, the odd deckchair that must have been found by the pool. It's a strange site for a military briefing. No one is in uniform any more — ours being too dirty — and everyone else seems to be dressed in black combat gear, whereas we only have our GDO army issue off-duty blues.

"It's good to see you all again, except you Dibsy." The other soldiers cheer and laugh and jostle someone who must be Dibsy. "Thanks to Sault squad, the Auria prison break was a success, and thanks to our teams on the ground in Auria, we're well on our way to reclaiming our first nation!"

The room erupts with cheers; this is what we're fighting for, to regain our independence from the GDO after they had systematically occupied every nation in Old Europe. Auria was the last country they invaded.

"Our next step is to re-take Troyes, and from there we can move on to Paris!" His voice is strong and deep and carries across the room, stirring something inside each of us. I also notice that he doesn't use the GDO names for the cities — Pradis is Paris and Senbur is Troyes. It's easier to follow what's happening when we use Old European names. Dune's voice begins to rise, knowing that the passion of the Resistance fighters is what will drive the movement forward; they need this hunger to succeed, to recapture the will of the people so that they will also support our cause.

When the room is a little calmer, he starts to speak again and everyone falls silent instantly. "We need the people on our side if we're to stand a chance of winning. I'll be sending in a team to start firing up support with civilians and we will start disrupting the GDO's plans." There are a few whoops in response to that. "We will intercept more of their arms shipments and any other supplies heading to their bases. *Disrupt and disarm.* Then we're going to feed in false intel so they think we're heading straight to Paris, let them think we're reckless and stupid." A few of the soldiers jeer at that. "And then, when they're looking the wrong way…" He leans forward, his face intense and fierce. "We strike and take back our first city." The room falls into a chaos of shouts and cheers. Dune has done his work; he's made them want to fight again, to fight for him. That's all he needs right now. Later he'll tell us all what's expected of us, but tonight — tonight we celebrate.

Four long tables have been laid out on the lawn between the barracks and the farmhouse. Tablecloths, which on closer inspection are a mixture of old bed sheets, throws, and possibly one or two actual tablecloths, flap gently in the breeze.

We sit down to fresh baguettes, rich and flavoursome cassoulet, and tartes aux pommes for dessert. And wine, real red wine. It is genuinely the best meal I think I've ever had.

"I'm so glad we ended up in France," Drummer sighs happily, as he drinks his wine.

"Way better food than in Auria," Jono states.

"Hey! We have good food too; you just caught us at a bad time," I protest.

"Like...?" Jono looks genuinely mystified.

"Venison stew," I offer.

"A stew can't be a national dish." Drummer sounds appalled.

"It's a good stew," Luca says, coming to Auria's defence.

"But it's stew!" Jono exclaims.

"What's the Welsh national dish? Cheese on toast?" I respond.

"Bara brith," Jono tells us.

"What the hell is a bara brith?" I ask.

"It's like a fruit cake," Jono replies, proudly.

"Fruit cake? You can't be rude about stew if you have fruit cake." I'm indignant at the slight.

"Bet you have a great traditional dish," Luca says to Shreya who has turned to us.

"We eat a lot of fish — ambot tik is probably one of the more well known, it's sort of sour tasting." Jono pulls a face. "I don't think you could handle it Jono — it's pretty spicy." Shreya smiles at him.

"Hey, I don't have fiery hair for nothing." He runs his hands through it for emphasis.

"No, you do, you literally have fiery hair for no reason. You cannot even handle a korma, mate." Jono looks stricken at Drummer's insult but quickly laughs it off.

It is nice to feel like a normal person again, instead of a soldier, even if it is only for one evening. It helps, but only a little because when I close my eyes to sleep the dead come to haunt me.

WEEK TWENTY-ONE

KOHLER

Kohler arrived at the facility and grimaced. Children. He was to be in charge of children.

"I think you'll find that they're very malleable."

"General, with the right methods, I think you'll find most people incredibly malleable." Kohler gives the general a meaningful look.

"And yet you were bettered by a seventeen year old."

Kohler stretched his neck backwards, jutting his chin out. "I underestimated her, a mistake I won't make again."

"I should hope not. Never underestimate your opponent, you should know that by now."

"Yes, General." Kohler couldn't look into the familiar cool blue eyes for long; instead, he turned to survey the room. It was a large chamber, with metal walls and ceilings that made it look almost like an aeroplane hangar. There were around two hundred children lined up, feet shoulder-width apart, hands clasped behind their backs, and wearing the off-duty blues of the GDO army.

"And what would you like me to do with this lot?" Kohler felt the goal he was reaching for slip a little further from him.

"They are to be our new army. Run drills, keep them fit... make them ruthless, lethal. Use that anger and make them the sharp point of our sword. No one will expect this from us; we can infiltrate all Resistance pockets with them."

"You think they're up to such a task?" Kohler looked at the adolescents before him with bemusement.

"We have one in place now, let me show you something." The general approached the drill sergeant and told him to carry on; he began to bark orders at the room filled with miniature soldiers. Kohler felt oddly unsettled by the sight; it felt a little too familiar for his liking, but he ignored the sensation — that was the past. Today he was going to change the pattern.

The general led him to another room, about half the size of the previous one with a white projection table and soldiers working at computers nearby. The general brought up a file on the table; it showed a 3D plan of a 'coms device.

"We've finally been able to test out the biotech we've been developing on the recruits we have here. Not only do the 'coms work exactly as we'd hoped, the Symbio programme has its first ever subject out in the field." He opened another file so there's a split screen, and two 3D models of implants rotated slowly on the screen.

"Symbio?"

"A classified project to link two soldiers together so that in the field they're a more effective team through seamless communication — they almost become one mind. We're also trialling some ocular implants to improve image transfer. Our best recruit is, right now, infiltrating a Resistance camp, and we have all the tech we need to communicate with her standard 'com implant and for her to transmit images. They will have no idea what they're dealing with."

"This is a turning point." Kohler felt his heart hammer with excitement. They were going to finally crush these ridiculous rebellions, and they would finally bring the peace and prosperity they'd long ago envisioned. The GDO was going save Old Europe; then it was going to reshape the world.

RAGE

It is early morning and Rage's legs are starting to cramp; she's been crouched behind a pile of rubble, rubbish, and scrap metal for a couple of hours. She's waiting until she feels the time is right. The sun needs to be up enough that the Resistance fighters will be awake, but she needs to time it so that they are still at their base.

She checks the wires one last time. She likes to make her own bombs; it's always better to be in full control of an explosion you're making, and that way you know how big it will be. She never calculates the blast radius by any complex mathematics — for Rage, it's all done on instinct. She knows, with each bomb, how big the blast is going to be. This one — this one is only a medium. It has been a while since she's created anything truly spectacular, which is a shame.

She judges the time to be right, so she creeps forward, places the bomb carefully by an old petrol pump that has begun to rust, and sets the timer. The shelter above has partially fallen away and light leaks over the area where she is standing. She quickly moves away not wanting to be seen, and then visualises the radius. How close is too close? She puts the clear wax in her ears, hoping her ear drums won't rupture. She stands in front of the pile of debris she had been hiding behind, before estimating that she'll be blown back against it, giving herself cuts and bruises. Hopefully she won't break anything; that will really hinder her spying.

She takes a deep breath and then whispers in her mind, *"Are you awake?"*

"Just about," comes the reply.

"I'm about to trigger the bomb." She holds back her fear, not letting Knight feel any of it.

"Be safe." She can feel his worry and it doesn't help her nerves.

"Always am." By convincing him, she can convince herself. She's done it before.

"I mean it, Rae; I need you around. You're not allowed to die because I need you, doesn't matter about you. You got that?"

Rage smiles. *"Yeah, I got that. I'll let you know when it's done."*

She waits three more seconds and then closes her eyes. This is going to hurt. The explosion rips through the air like a violent scream with jagged fingers, throwing her backwards, tearing at her clothes, her flesh, singeing her hair. Her back slams into a large jagged stone, just to the right of her spine. The pain makes her eyes water. She is scorched all over, scraped and bloodied, aching and coughing.

"Shit."

"You're alive then?"

"Just."

"Oh good, now I can go back to sleep."

Rage lets out a surprised laugh and feels her lip split. "Ow," she scowls, and the 'com link at the base of her skull transmits the mood to Knight.

"I felt that," Knight responds.

"Good." Rage lays her head back against an old piece of a metal door panel and closes her eyes, waits. The rock is still digging into her back, her skin stinging, but she doesn't move. Make it believable, they'd said. And so she does.

CASSIA

My head whips round at the explosion. Fire dances in my mind and goose bumps rise all over my arms. Not another explosion… Jake's face, his t-shirt, the one I used to sleep in, bunched up, just before…

I force myself to focus and look around. We're dressed in our new black combat uniforms and are waiting for our first full briefing as a team. Dune marches into what was once the farmhouse's living room.

"Sault team, come with me — we're checking out the explosion." We run to grab our packs, helmets, and rifles and set out slowly down winding path towards the main road where smoke is now curling lazily upwards.

I don't want to walk towards an explosion. I'm losing my battle to stay focused; I want this to stop, and I want to feel like myself again. I don't want to be afraid and unfocused. I need to stop. And then I do stop, because we're at the site of the explosion. Flames are still lapping up the side of the petrol station's main building, smoke still thick in the air. Dune makes us fan out, expecting an ambush, preparing for anything. Only once the smoke starts to clear do I see her, a little girl. Her dark hair has fallen to cover part of her face, which is marred with tiny cuts and burn marks from the blast. Her baby-pink t-shirt with a big sparkly star in the middle is ripped, and most of the sequins have melted in on themselves. I run to her. Dune shouts something about checking the area first, but I'm moving on instinct. She can't be dead, she can't be. Not another one. I can't cope with another one.

My heart is hammering so hard now that it physically hurts. I reach her and kneel down, laying my rifle in front of me and softly taking her hand to feel for a pulse. It's there and it's strong. I let out a breath, unshoulder my pack, and pull out a water canteen. I brush her hair from her face, feeling her breath across my hand, and gently dribble a little water into her mouth. Her lips move sluggishly and then part. She opens her eyes slowly, painfully, and I'm surprised by how blue they are, assuming they'd be brown. She blinks once, twice, and then looks at me and begins to cry. I wipe away her tears and give her more water, and then get her to try and move her fingers and feet — she's not paralysed and I could almost cry myself with relief. Luca kneels down next to me and gives her a reassuring smile. Slowly and carefully, we help her stand. The back of her t-shirt is a mess of bloody marks but none of them appear too deep, but they're likely very painful.

"We need to get her checked out; she may have internal damage from the impact against the rubble." Luca looks at me and I nod in confirmation. "We'll stretcher her to minimise any further damage."

Dune comes over after having examined the blast site. "Good idea — Jono, Drummer, rig a stretcher." Dune looks around; Shreya and Yve are standing sentry at the furthest points of the blast radius. "Single detonation, possibly to draw us out. Let's get moving."

We work quickly to help the girl onto the stretcher and make our way back to camp. Dune takes point with Jono who has a metal detector, checking for any anti-personnel mines, moving as quickly as we can. I'm heading up the rear with Yve and so I can't stay with the child. Luca's helping to carry her on the stretcher and he's talking to her, reassuring her, trying to find out her name. She doesn't say a single word, and just cries and shakes.

Back at the farmhouse, the little girl is taken into the med building, an old holiday cottage a little further out on the property that affords the doctor and patients some privacy. I elect to stay with her whilst she's examined by the doctor, but every time he goes to touch her she flinches away.

"I can't help you if you won't let me see your injuries." The doctor is gentle but the little girl remains reluctant.

"No, I'm okay, thank you."

"Are you sure? You suffered quite the impact." He looks at her with concern.

"I think it's just bruises," she says in a small voice.

"Is there anything we need to be concerned about?" I ask the doctor.

"It all seems superficial. A shower, some iodine on the worst cuts, and I can give her some painkillers for the extensive bruising. Otherwise, she'll feel better in a few days."

I thank the doctor and lead the girl to the mess, picking up a spare t-shirt and trousers on the way. I wait inside the bathroom as she showers with the curtain drawn. I feel bad for invading her privacy but I know not to let her out of my sight. She dresses in the clothes I had managed to find for her, but the t-shirt hangs past her knees and the trousers are so big it's not even worth rolling them up.

"We'll have to get you some new clothes." I'm sitting on the floor as I fold up the trousers and I sigh as I take her in. Where on earth had she come from? There shouldn't be anyone for miles around; it doesn't make any sense. "What are you doing on your own out here?" I ask gently.

Her big eyes fill with tears. "I was lost… My… my…" She gulps down her tears. "Mummy, she d-d-died." There's nothing I can say to make her pain any less, and so instead I hold her gently until she's cried out. She feels so small and fragile in my arms. When she's recovered, I ask how the explosion happened.

"I saw some soldiers and so I hid from them but they found me and made me stand at gun point and then they set a bomb and made me stand there with a gun in my face and then they started walking away but the gun was still in my face and then the bomb exploded." Her eyes are wide and a fat tear falls down her cheek and onto the floor. I remember what it's like to be held at gunpoint by the GDO, and I can finally feel the familiar burn of anger in my core. I can feel my purpose returning.

WEEK TWENTY-TWO

RAGE

So far, Rage is pretty happy with how things have been going. The sappy girl called Cassia seems to have taken pity on her, giving her those puppy-dog eyes when she tells her some stupid sad story. But now she's sitting in front of the one who seems to be in charge, Dune. A woman with red hair is also in the room, staring at her, and the younger woman, Cassia, sits next to her.

Rage doesn't like the one with red hair — she's used to people trying to intimidate her and so it doesn't bother her, but she also doesn't like that it reminds her of the people who have intimidated her in the past. The man, who to Rage seems pretty old, gives her a level and honest stare. Surprisingly, she likes the directness of his gaze.

"What's your name?"

She's about to say Rage and then realises that the name she chose for herself all those years ago may just give the game away. "Rae," she offers instead. She doesn't like using the nickname that only Knight uses, but it's the first thing that comes to her mind because he's currently humming to himself, a habit he has when he's working on a particularly challenging algorithm, and it's making it hard for her to think.

"How long have you been lost, Rae?"

"I don't know." She looks to Cassia to act as though she needs reassurance. Cassia reaches out and holds her hand. Perfect.

"How many nights were you alone?"

"Th-three," she says, and pulls at the oversized t-shirt.

"And before that, was it just you and your mother?"

Rage nods and keeps her eyes down, locking her ankles together to show intimidation.

"Can you describe the soldiers who chased you?"

"There was three of them." She winced inwardly; did she sound too young, then? Was her voice too whiny? She couldn't lose focus. She spoke to Knight. *"How do I get them on my side?"*

"Have you tried crying?"

"I'm dehydrated from all the bloody crying."

"Try mutism, kinda works for me." Rage's heart squeezes at that; she knows Knight would talk to her if he could.

"It's too late for that."

"Maybe they'll want to protect an innocent child, on instinct or something."

And then she had the answer. "One of them stroked my hair and said he wanted me to keep him company but I didn't like him and I didn't want to go with them and that's why I kept running." Cassia's hand tightens on hers. Dune sits back.

"She can't stay here." His response sounds more like a reflex than anything else. Rage begins to feel unease uncurling in her stomach. Dune is a man in control and she hasn't had great experiences with them in the past. She wonders why her first instinct was to trust him; it was a foolish impulse.

"But she can stay temporarily, until we can find a family to take her in?" Rage can tell Cassia is trying not to sound too pleading; she must respect Dune if she doesn't want to push him. The redhead stays silent — she might become a problem.

"Fine, she sleeps in the farmhouse, though, I don't want her in the barracks."

"Thank you."

The redhead watches Rage as she leaves and the back of her neck prickles, right where her implant scar is.

Cassia introduces Rage to her friends and they sit down for lunch together and talk about what their mission might be. This is good, Rage thinks; they aren't being wary around her. She sends a 'com to base confirming that she's securely embedded in a large Resistance camp. She decides she likes Cassia's friends — they don't act like normal soldiers, and even Cassia doesn't seem so bad now she's stopped worrying over her. Her boyfriend Luca is pretty handsome, too, Rage supposes. She doesn't really pay much attention usually to these things but with him, it's hard to miss. He seems too gentle to be a soldier, too aware of everyone around him, how they are doing. But then again, no one there would take her for a soldier either. She wonders if he, too, has a savage side.

The team is called in for a briefing after lunch and so Rage is left to her own devices. She considers listening in, but that's not a smart move in the middle of the day when there are people everywhere. Instead she familiarises herself with the base and sends snapshot images through her 'com link by blinking three times in quick succession, her optic implants taking care of the rest. She can see where their supplies are stored when the barn is opened up for someone to enter, and she makes a note to investigate it at night. Then she goes into the mess hall and sits in the corner and waits, quietly, making herself almost invisible to the soldiers coming and going, allowing her to listen in on their conversations. She gathers snippets of information —some raids are going ahead, one group is heading out to try to fire up support nearby, but she doesn't catch the name of the location. Everything that seems of importance she feeds back to base.

She continues to watch and listen.

KOHLER

Major Kohler monitored the information as it trickled in from the asset at the Resistance camp. Nothing solid enough to go on, yet. But soon — soon he'd have something.

He was sitting in his new office, a small window looking out onto a concrete courtyard, the walls blank, his only items a chair, desk, and computer. It didn't look like much, but he could tell that this small space symbolised his status, and symbols were important.

Yes, he'd thought, maybe being here is better for his position in the GDO, to be part of the advanced programme instead of sitting around looking after an inconsequential town in a country that its own people, unbelievably, had begun to re-take. Sometimes the naivety of the Aurians angered him, and then he recalled that people were just far too stuck in their ways, unable to see that the new system was better, safer.

What was the saying, he mused, as he looked around his new seat of power. Oh yes, *You can't make an omelette without breaking a few eggs.*

WEEK TWENTY-THREE

CASSIA

Being at the farmhouse has given us far more of an idea of the Resistance's reach, of how big it has grown. Dune briefs us on the other units across Old France and the rest of Old Europe. There is something thrilling about the idea that we are part of this movement against the regime, a small cog in a giant machine, working towards positive change. I feel pride as he takes us through the structure and explains that the main cell is based in Utonia, the GDO's capital, once known as Spain. I remember going on holiday to the southern coast when I was about ten, eating fresh fried fish on the beach by a huge outdoor barbeque, trying to find crabs with my dad whilst my mum watched on, smiling. And now it's where the heart of our enemy lies. The place where we will all finally go to end this.

Dune has tasked us with intercepting an arms delivery to a base twenty miles out. Fortunately for us, Clive is doing an amazing job of supplying us with intel on GDO movements. I think he's enjoying being integrated into the Resistance intelligence network and working for our unit. He says it makes him feel like he's part of an underground spy ring, like in an action film. I suppose, in a way, he is. He's hacked into the GDO system for us, saying it's thanks to the stuff I found when working for GDO intelligence, but I'm sure he's just saying that to be nice. It was more fluke than real skill that made me find the files on SINN, the GDO's internal network. I just hope that he's safe in his basement in Auria, because what he's doing for us could get him killed, although everything we do now comes with that risk.

When we leave our briefing I feel unusually light; the prospect of intercepting weapons from the GDO is exactly what I want to be doing — taking from them so they can no longer take from us. Actions like this are the reason I joined the Resistance. I smile at Luca and he looks at me with surprise, then picks me up and plants an enthusiastic kiss on my lips.

Luca and I go and look for Rae. I hope that she's okay as she really didn't seem ready to be left alone, but I have to follow orders. Eventually Yve finds her in the mess and we join her.

"So kid, fancy playing a game? We're stuck here until dark." Yve cocks her head to one side, almost as a challenge to Rae. Some of her old rebelliousness is coming back to her.

Rae looks at me expectantly. "We could play sleeping lions, it's my favourite game," I offer.

"That's because you like sleeping." Luca rolls his eyes at me. "No, let's play something more energetic."

Pranav walks into the mess. "You talking about playing a game?"

"Yeah," I say, and turn to him.

"Oh, I've got a great one we can all play."

"Age appropriate?" I ask, and incline my head towards Rae.

"Absolutely," he grins, and I'm suddenly a little wary about what his game is.

Pranav stands in the middle of a ring of soldiers who are all waiting for nightfall for their missions to begin. He raises his hands in the air. "Today, ladies and gentlemen, we play… Human Hungry Hippos *with a twist!*"

He divides us into two teams — one team are the hippos, the other, the lions. He's raided the storeroom and has taken wheeled flatbed dollies for the hippos. The hippos are made up of pairs who have to wheelbarrow each other around. One person lies on the cart and the other holds their legs and manoeuvers them around. The person lying down has a container of some sort — there are cooking pots, mixing bowls, helmets — and they have to collect the prize, which is a pile rotting apples from the farm's orchard. The lions have to stop us, the Hippos, from getting food and bringing it back to our base (an area marked off with our packs) where it's safe. The lions are also in pairs — they're tied together so that they're running three legged. Their hands are also tied behind their backs so that they can only try to grab our food with their mouths.

I team up with Rae, who selects a cooking pot with two handles as she thinks it'll be easier to hold on to. She looks excited to be playing the game. Luca is on the opposing team and is paired with Drummer, who gives me a mischievous grin — he's coming for us. The hippos and lions are at either end of the lawn; the apples are in the middle. I hold on to Rae's feet. Pranav is the bottom of the barrow next to me, and he winks at Rae and then the game begins.

Rae puts a pot on her head and moves us forward with surprising speed. The other hippos follow suit; it's too hard to move forward otherwise. We're the first to the apples on our team because Rae is so light and quick, but some of the lions are already there. She goes down onto her elbows and pulls the pot off her head, and then Luca dives forward, head first, trying to get the pot on his head to take it from us and take us out of the game. Rae clonks him over the head with it and he pulls back, surprised — I'm laughing at the shock on his face but Rae is dragging apples into the pot, biting her lip with determination.

"Go, go, go!" she yells, and I turn us around. The pot is now upside down on the grass, the only way we're allowed to transport our food. I'm having to push Rae along the grass, whilst holding onto her t-shirt so she doesn't flash everyone. She's laughing now, too, and her body is shaking because of it, making it almost impossible to push her. There's a roar behind me and I'm pounced on from behind. I collapse to the ground under the weight of Yve and Jono. Jono grabs for the bucket with his head and bites down on a rotting apple and instantly spits it out, yelling in disgust. He tries to get up, pulling Yve with him, but they can't because we're all tangled together. I yell at Rae, "Run! Save yourself," and she belly crawls to the drop site and slides our apples into the den. Rae jumps and does a little victory dance — Yve and Jono untangle themselves and swear at me. Such sore losers.

Rae and I are now out of the game because, technically, we're dead. We watch from the sidelines as Pranav floors Luca and Drummer by tripping them up, and I catch the look between Pranav and Drummer — a secret smile that speaks volumes. All the hippos are now out, so it's time to count up the food to see who won. Rae and I sidle over to the leftover apples and surreptitiously collect a few and then fling them off into a flower bed.

"And the winner is…" Pranav yells with glee, "Hippos, with a margin of three apples!"

Rae beams up at me conspiratorially.

The light is fading fast and so we have to shake off our jubilation and focus on prepping for our mission.

"Are you going to be safe?" Rae asks me as she helps me load up my pack.

Luca's packing next to me, all his things laid out on his bed. "She's got me to keep her safe."

Rae screws up her face. "Somehow I think she's in safer hands with Jono."

Luca barks out a surprised laugh. "I think you should have come with a warning," Luca says.

"We'll be fine, you don't have to worry about a thing, and I'm sure Dune will keep you company whilst we're out."

"He's not going?"

"He's Command," I say with an ominous voice. "Echo, Dune, Ham, and Ian will stay here and coordinate all the different operations."

"Why is everyone going tonight?" she asks innocently, her brow furrowed.

"It's always better to show your hand in one go, take the enemy by surprise." Rae nods sagely, as if she understands battle strategies.

A soldier whose name I don't know yet enters our room. "Sault team, your truck is ready."

We file out of the barracks and climb into the back of the vehicle — we're to be dropped off a mile from our interception point and picked up just before dawn if we fail to procure the GDO's transport. Rae waves goodbye to us as we pull away. She looks so small, so vulnerable. I just hope she'll be okay.

RAGE

As Rage is watching Sault team leave, Knight speaks to her.

"How's it going?" She can feel his apprehension even though he manages to keep it out of the tone of his question.

"We played a game." She tries to be nonchalant about it. It wouldn't be fair to rub it in his face.

"A game?!" Knight's surprise is evident. *"When's the last time we played a game?"*

"Before."

"Yeah… before." He hesitates before speaking. *"You like them."*

"Yeah, but that don't matter. I have a mission."

"But Rae—"

"I've got a mission, Knight."

"They're the good guys, though." Even though they know each other on the inside, she can feel his shyness at speaking up.

"There's no such thing as good guys and bad guys, you know that. There's just survival and we're gonna survive this. Got it?" She didn't want to put him down but she couldn't have him thinking like that — it was too much of a risk.

"Yeah, I got it, Rae… I miss you."

"Miss you, too, Knight. Miss you, too." Rage turns to the compound and makes her way to the storage building; it's time to get to work. But before she is even half way to the building, Echo intercepts her.

"How's our youngest member getting on?" She cocks her head to the side, a smile dancing on her lips.

"Playing a hippo was fun," Rae says with a shy smile.

"Best thing about this army is hanging out with your buddies."

"It's pretty cool."

"Sure is." Echo is frowning slightly, like there's something bothering her. "How about we hang out tomorrow, I need to get back and my head's already bothering me." She rubs her temple absently and Rage smiles.

"I'd like that."

"Good. Stay out of trouble." Echo heads off towards the main farmhouse and Rage slips into the shadows as she makes for the outer buildings. As the dark settles in around her, whilst she waits to inch forward through the door, she can't help remembering her time with the GDO.

The first time she ran away she was only seven years old. She had been at the GDO base for nearly eight months, and her birthday had been and gone without her noticing. She'd been in solitary confinement for two weeks, punished for stealing an extra piece of bread for the tiny boy who looked like he was starving, who always sat in the corner, shaking and filthy.

She didn't like the dark before she went into solitary. When she was released, she hated the dark. Hated, hated, hated it. She didn't want to be in the dark again; she didn't understand why it was so wrong to feed the starving boy and so she decided to run away. It was surprisingly easy. They didn't expect a seven-year-old to try to escape, or even succeed. She made it past the wire fence and into the woods before they caught her. That was the site of her first proper beating. Everything before then had merely been lashings, sharp stings of pain to keep her in line, but they were over so quickly they weren't worth fearing. The beating was harder not to fear. The pain afterwards lasted for days and days. She couldn't cut her own food; she would end up starved like the dirty little boy. She sat and stared at her food, wanting to cry and not wanting them to see her cry, already wanting to resist them. The little boy came out of the corner for the first time, sat down next to her, and slowly cut her food for her, and when she couldn't lift her fork to her mouth to feed herself, he did it for her.

From that moment on, he was her Knight.

CASSIA

Bumping along dusty lanes in the back of a truck, I'm reminded of our escape from prison — Dune coming to rescue Luca and me from execution even though he'd never met us. It seems like it was so long ago, but it must only have been a month now. Shreya's sitting next to me but I don't try to talk to her — what's the point? She's determined to dislike me and like everybody else. I close my eyes and drift into sleep but wake up soon after when another nightmare chases me down. I had thought I was improving but I'm still haunted; I suppose that a single afternoon of feeling normal doesn't mean all my fears have magically vanished. Shreya gives me a sidelong look.

"You getting nightmares?" she asks.

"A few," I reply offhandedly, as if they don't really bother me, despite my pulse having quadrupled.

"I do, too, sometimes." She says this quietly, as though she doesn't want to admit something like that to me.

"I guess most of us do."

"Yeah, I guess."

That's all we say to each other for the whole journey, but it makes me think that maybe she doesn't hate me so much after all. Yve smiles at me from the opposite bench as if to say, *See, it'll work itself out.*

When the jeep stops, making as little noise as we can, we climb out and crouch down until it leaves. Luca's in command for this mission, and so we follow his lead as we stand and begin walking towards our ambush point. We make our way around a tight bend, unable to see the road beyond; it is there, where the road straightens out once again, that we will hide. Either side of us are trees, thickly sentried along the road and stretching into the forest on either side. On the furthest side of the road is a bank covered in long grass that stretches upwards towards the trees.

We're all in black. We are wearing our Resistance combat trousers, black boots, black jackets, black packs. We operate at night mostly, so the choice in colour makes sense, although, secretly, I prefer the GDO off-duty blues.

We reach our destination in silence, and Luca divides us up into pairs so that we're covering different points in pairs on the road. Yve and I hunker down in a ditch whilst Jono and Drummer run spikes across the road. Now all we need to do is wait.

"This is my least favourite part," Yve whispers to me.

"Waiting around — yeah, me too."

"No, needing to pee and not knowing if it's okay to go now or just wait it out and potentially, accidentally, wet yourself in the excitement of the moment."

"Oh… yeah, that's not great. Go here, I'll cover you… just, don't get any on my boots."

"We better switch places then so I'm not standing higher than you."

"Good point."

We switch and I stand guard as Yve drops her trousers. I'm tempted to tell her the GDO are approaching just to make her jump, but I'm worried that in her panic she'll splash me. When she's done, I wonder how long it'll be before my legs begin to cramp. Fortunately, I don't have to wait long before a convoy of vehicles approaches.

Further up the road, Jono is waiting, acting as our group's eyes. He radios in. "There's more than one truck, there are three, what do we do? There aren't enough of us…" I look over to Luca who's clearly calculating the odds.

Jono continues on. "None are holding troops by the looks of things — two up front, possibly additional guards in the back."

My palms start to sweat — this is bad. We need the supplies and we need to begin our plan of disrupting the GDO, but if we play this wrong we could all end up dead or captured, and I'm not sure which would be more preferable.

"Luca?" Yve asks.

"I'm thinking," he whispers down his radio mic. "Cass…"

"Dune would be fine with it if we walk away, we can't risk everyone here," I assure him.

"I agree. Drummer, pull the spikes back."

Drummer begins to do as Luca instructs, but halfway across the road the spikes snag on something. He tugs as hard as he can but to no avail. The front of the convey is seconds away.

"Looks like we're going to have to do this," Luca says hastily through his 'com. "Shreya and I will take the middle truck. Jono, you need to get down here and join Drummer in taking the rear, Yve and Cass take the front one."

Drummer sniggers at the innuendo but quickly sobers. "Yes, boss."

Because the spikes are over only half the road, the front right tyre of the first vehicle blows and it skids off to one side, the truck closest behind careening into it. We wait for them to stop moving before we approach and in that time, I think about how I've been the cause of a lot of deaths but I've never shot anyone point blank. That is about to change. Dune had let us keep our electroshock guns, but both my hands are on my rifle. We can't take any chances right now. I may have to kill someone today.

As the GDO vehicles screech to a stop, we run from our hiding spots and I wish that we had another team with us, because we are not prepared to take on a convoy, but we have to try. However, I don't think about that. If I think about that, I'll freeze up and Yve needs me.

Simultaneously, Yve and I reach opposite sides of the truck, slamming our feet down onto the steps that go up into the cab. We fling the doors open, and as I pull the soldier in the passenger seat down, the momentum throws him to the ground. I train my rifle at his head and kick his gun off to the side. I hear a scuffle from the other side and call out to Yve.

"I'm good." Only then do I look up. Luca and Shreya have secured their targets but three more soldiers have burst from the back of the last vehicle and Jono and Drummer are now outnumbered 5:2. I tie the soldier's arms behind his back and look through the sight on my rifle; Yve comes over to my side of the truck and raises hers also. My heart is hammering because the way things are going; I know what the next order is going to be. Sweat makes my hands slick, but I don't dare wipe them for fear I'll miss my moment. Luca shouts to the men who now have Jono and Drummer on their knees to put their weapons down, but I can tell they're not going to listen to him. Shreya and Luca are closer, but Yve and I are in a better position.

"We've got clear sight," Yve says in a whisper into her headset. Her face is set with determination and there is anger bright and clear in her eyes. Her hatred of the GDO, of everything they do and stand for radiates off her in this moment. This must be what an avenging angel looks like.

"Take the shot," Luca orders, and in that moment I hate him, but I know my choices and losing Jono and Drummer isn't something I'm going to risk. I pull the trigger. The bullet rips through the soldier's left shoulder; Yve's goes straight through the other soldier's right eye.

Shreya and Luca fire and take down the other two soldiers at the same time, and the fifth Yve gets in her sights and shoots in the chest. My attention catches on Luca as he fires. To see him act in this way feels strange; he seems almost alien to me. Always the gentle soul, and yet this war has turned him into something other than who he was. He is not worse for it, just braver, stronger than I will ever be. It has turned him into a weapon, but a weapon that is only wielded when absolutely necessary.

We don't stop to think. Our training keeps us moving and we go through each of the vehicles checking for more soldiers whilst Luca stands on guard with Yve. As I pass Luca, he gives me a look — one of disappointment because I didn't shoot to kill, which could have cost Jono his life. I didn't think I'd be a liability to the team but maybe, after all that's happened, that's all I'll ever be — never quite the soldier.

Dune had instructed us to dispose of bodies and bring back anyone we could capture. What you don't realise until you're next to a dead body is that when they die, every part of the body relaxes and they reek of faeces, which makes an unpleasant job even more horrible. Drummer and Luca haul our captives into the back of a truck, and Yve is put in charge of guarding them, having shown herself capable of taking the necessary measures. The rest of us carefully carry the dead bodies into a clearing. I'm able to hold down my nausea, but only just. I'm disgusted that we're having to abandon these men, who are loved by someone, to wild animals, to decay out in the open like this. I think back to the piles of bodies we covered and hate that we are hypocrites in this, just because a uniform deems us enemies. I take care to straighten them up before we leave, to give them some dignity in their death.

We have to change the tyre of the front truck before we can go anywhere, which takes a lot longer than we would have liked, but we manage it and Luca and I take the front truck, leading the convoy back to the farmhouse.

After a long silence, I pluck up the courage to speak. "You're angry with me."

"Not angry, it's just…" He doesn't want to say it — doesn't want to say that I should have killed the GDO soldier, because how would that make him sound?

"I put Jono at risk," I say, quietly.

"Yeah, but it all worked out, so it doesn't matter." He smiles at me and I begin to feel really angry with him.

"Can you just stop?"

"Stop what?"

"Pitying me! Treating me like I'm too fragile to criticise! I put Jono's life in danger because I don't have it in me to kill someone else when it really matters. We're at war and it's us or them and yet, I still can't do it." I can't face him and so I turn to the window.

"I don't fault you for that, I love you for that." I can hear some tension in his voice, though.

"But you don't, I saw your face, you were disappointed in me!" Tears fill my eyes.

"I never said that, you're making assumptions." I dab the tears away before they fall, trying to pull myself together.

"Just say what you really feel." I cross my arms and turn to glare at him.

"Okay, fine, it worked out in this situation, but I'm scared that one day it's going to be between you or someone else and you'll end up dying because you don't want to cross that line. We're at war, Cassia, no one wants to step over that line. Even after the first time it's going to continue to be difficult, but we signed up to fight for our people, for the people of Old Europe. We have to make the tough choices." He grips the steering wheel tighter, even now trying to reign in his temper.

"Don't you think I've made enough tough choices?!" I yell at him.

"Then why did you come?! Why didn't you stay in Vayo?! You didn't have to join the Resistance, Cass, but you made that choice, no one asked you to." He glances at me and I finally feel the full weight of his anger.

I'm seething now. "What kind of choice was I left with? Stay in Vayo and do nothing or try and make a difference?"

"Yes, you could have stayed, and then I wouldn't have to constantly worry about you."

"It's not your job to worry about me," I snap.

"Of course it is, I love you, I'm going to worry about you, but I need to know that if it comes to it you won't hesitate, that you'll shoot to kill. I can't lose you, Cass." His hands relax as his anger begins to leave him. "Seeing what Jake's death and the GDO's retaliation has done to you... it's hard on me, too."

"I know." I can't look at him. I feel too much guilt. "If it comes to it, I won't hesitate. Do you know why?"

"No."

"Because I'd never do that to you."

Luca takes in a shaky breath. "Oh, so you are a romantic after all."

I laugh through tears, which seem to have appeared from nowhere. "Who wouldn't kill for you, Luca Kemei?"

His smile is big as he takes my hand. We drive back to the farmhouse like that, only letting go for him to change gear. But, the truth is, I don't know if I wouldn't hesitate — for Luca's sake, I don't want to die. I don't want to inflict that pain on him. But, even so... I don't know if I wouldn't hesitate. I don't know.

KOHLER

Major Kohler stood in front of a group of twenty recruits; they were the newer intakes to the programme. Some looked puffy eyed from a night of crying, others seemed confused. Despite himself, he found he was unsettled by his new role — training children to become soldiers wasn't what he had in mind when he thought of climbing the military ranks. He pushed his distaste aside and focused on his own goal instead.

"Do you know why the Global Defence Organisation was formed?" He looked around at the room but they were all too afraid to speak — the eldest was only twelve, the youngest seven.

He spoke louder, showing his authority. "To bring peace to Old Europe. Nearly seven years ago there was an uprising. The people were unhappy with their government and the government couldn't control its people, and so the GDO was formed to help bring peace to nations who couldn't do it themselves. And then more riots happened, and the GDO had to go and help stop those, too. We got bigger and stronger and we saw what was really wrong. The people of Old Europe were all *unhappy*, there was no *unity* anymore — after the first state left the union, the discontent and mistrust spread like a disease. The GDO was the cure." There still wasn't much of a response, of any kind, from the children.

"Have any of you ever had an injection?" There were a few nods. "Well, an injection is preventative medicine, it stops you getting an illness. One day the GDO realised that all that unrest was going to spread, and so we decided to take preventative measures and we took control, gradually, of every nation in Old Europe so that one day, there would be *peace* and *prosperity* across our great continent once more."

Kohler looked around the room, taking in the confused and bewildered faces, and wondered if he'd ever be able to make them into soldiers. "And anyone who doesn't want peace has to be bad, because peace is a good thing, isn't it?" A few of the children nodded. "It's your job to help us bring an end to all the badness that has infected Old Europe. You're going to be the cure. Doesn't that sound like a noble thing to do?" A few more children nod this time. "Good. Now that you understand, it's time for your training. Today we're going to be doing circuits, because to beat the bad you have to be stronger."

Kohler stood with his hands behind his back watching as the children performed star jumps, jump squats, burpees, jump lunges, and skipping until a few of them were sick. Only then did he allow them to stop. He left the room, telling them to clean it up then meet him in the communications training room in 20 minutes, after they'd showered. As he walked away, he tried not to think of those strained, scared faces; he contemplated instead the greater good and his personal ambition. But a memory came unbidden of an early morning in the cold, being forced to do sprints when he was eight years old, and every time he had to stop, he was made to do ten more, and then being sick and sick and sick. He swallowed the memory down and prepared for training the recruits.

RAGE

She waits for the return of Cassia and the others, taking only snatches of sleep, having set her 'com to wake her every hour and, when it's nearly sunrise, she gets out of bed and waits in the shadows for Sault team's return. Just after dawn she sees three trucks approaching — she makes her way into the farmhouse and sneaks into the small briefing room, which was likely once the study of the house, and hides inside the cabinet of the dresser. She is beginning to realise why the GDO want children as soldiers — so they could hide in small spaces.

Just when she is starting to worry that they will debrief in a different room, the door opens and the team files in.

"How many were there?" It sounds to Rage as though Dune is speaking.

"Nine." She recognises the deep timber of Luca's voice.

"Well done for bringing five captives in, it'll be good to have them for questioning but you shouldn't have risked attacking such a large number with only your team," Dune reprimands Luca.

"We were going to abort the mission but unfortunately the spikes became stuck and so we had no choice but to go ahead." Rage is impressed that Luca isn't apologising to Dune.

"Very well. And did you manage to check the cargo?"

"Briefly. The first two were weapons and supplies... the third, well, Jono — want to tell them what you found?"

"Some kind of tech..." There's a pause and Rage assumes it's Jono handing Dune a sample of what they had found. "It was in the truck that contained the guards. Whatever this stuff is, it's important to them."

Tech — Rage thinks, frantically. Could they have come across the GDOs 'coms implants, or even the Symbio ones? She sends a message immediately to base and receives a reply she doesn't like — "Destroy the tech." She expects some kind of disciplinary action for not warning them of the attack, but apparently she'll get to wait for that in person. Maybe if she steals some painkillers before she leaves it won't hurt too much.

"Knight?"

"Yeah?"

"Any ideas on how to destroy a bunch of tech the Resistance found, without making it look like it was done on purpose?" Rage shifts slightly to ease her cramped legs.

"Remove the nano chips and they won't be able to work them."

"Okay…" Rage rolls her eyes. *"How do I remove the nano chips?"*

"I'll upload a data file onto your 'com."

Urgh, really, can't you talk me through it?"

"Sorry, you'll need to see it."

Rage groaned internally. They still haven't quite mastered the viewing of files whilst 'com linked so that you don't feel like you're sea sick. The image comes through jumpy and makes your head swim. She'll have to endure it, though, if she's to carry out orders. She closes her eyes and watches the file, taking slow and steady breaths and hoping she doesn't vomit inside the cupboard, otherwise she's sure to be found out.

"Store the stuff in here for the time being until we can get them a secure lockup. I have a feeling these could be a game changer," Dune says. Rage hears everyone leave and then each gradually return, and soon she can hear what sounds like the team stacking boxes.

She waits, hoping no one has noticed she's missing, and when she feels the coast is clear, she slowly opens the door to her hiding space, gratefully stretching her aching limbs out into the now empty room.

Before opening the first box, she makes a mental note of how everything is stacked, and then when she looks inside the first container, how everything is packed inside. The best way to ensure you're not caught is to make sure nothing is out of place. There are five boxes and about twenty implants in each.

"This is going to take me forever — can't I use a magnet to mess up their wiring or something?"

"Doesn't work like that." She can hear the smile in his response.

"Shit, I don't know how I'm going to get this done without being caught. Any other brilliant ideas? I can't exactly burn the place down."

"Just... get started."

"Fine." She sends him a mental middle finger, not that he can *see* it, but he will definitely register the sentiment.

Extracting the nano chip on the first one is really fiddly and tricky, but by the fifth she's starting to get the hang of it. She's already taken 45 minutes, though. It's going too slowly. She 'coms her supervisor and tells them she'll need the camp distracted if she's going to get everything disabled. She keeps working until she's removed the chips from all the devices in one box. She shoves them into the pocket of her now washed, but ripped, jeans. She closes up the box and peaks through the key hole — the hall is empty. She opens the door just as Echo is walking down the corridor. She stops and looks at Rage, her brow furrowed.

"What are you up to?"

Rage's heart is hammering. How could she have been so careless? The chips inside her pocket feel like they're bulging out.

"Jus' wonderin' where everyone is?"

"In the mess, I'd have thought." Echo puts her hands in her pocket and betrays herself with a small smile. "Were you snooping?"

Rage hangs her head. "I jus' wanted to see what they got."

"And?" she shrugs.

"Some small plastic things." Rage tries to sound disappointed.

"Hoping for guns?" Echo arches her right eyebrow.

"Or a grenade or somethin'," Rage confesses, peeking up at Echo through her eyelashes. Her heartbeat starts to slow as she realises she might actually get away with it.

Echo holds in a smile. "You're lucky Dune didn't catch you snooping, otherwise you'd have been dropped off at the nearest town. However, if I catch you again it's bathroom cleaning duty… that includes after curry night *and* pulling the hair out of the plug holes."

Rage grimaces. "I won't snoop no more."

Echo leaves her, and relieved, Rage makes her way out and heads towards the kitchen and walks in, shyly.

"Hey kid, what can I do for you?" the cook asks. He is old, like Dune, wearing long shorts and a t-shirt, and she notices he has prosthetics on both legs.

"I, ummm, was wondering if I could help at all. I've got nothing to do."

"Sure, shrimp, why don't you peel some of them spuds?" He points to a bowl of potatoes.

Rage screws up her nose. "Isn't that usually a punishment?"

"If that's the case then I've been in trouble for a long time." He smiles at her and she notices his front tooth is cracked.

"What happened to your tooth?"

"Head-butted the table a few weeks back after a few too many of my home-brew ciders."

"You make cider here?" Rage grins up at him.

"Oh ho! I can see you're going to be trouble. And nice one, too."

"Nice one?"

"For asking about the tooth and not the legs."

"What legs?" Rage asks, her eyes wide with confusion. The cook, Carl, howls with laughter at her joke.

"Oh, I like you, kid. Go start peeling them spuds for later. If you do a good job I'll keep you on as my sous chef."

Rage gets to work on the potatoes, wondering when she could risk returning to the debriefing room, when she receives a 'com from base — she is to pick up a device from a dead-drop, a short-wave EMP that will permanently disable the tech.

"But what about my own tech?" she asks, panicking.

"There's a timer, you need to be at least 100 feet away."

"Is the timer one I'll be used to?"

"It's self-explanatory." Rage is getting increasingly frustrated. This is not helpful.

"How close will the device need to be to the tech?"

"Less than two metres."

"I'll retrieve it tonight."

And so, as she sits and peels potatoes, she goes over every exit she's noticed, every guard placement, and makes her plan.

Rage is unable to get back into the briefing room, and so accepts she'll have to wait until dark to get the EMP device. After their evening meal, Rage helps to clear up and tells Yve she's tired from a long day and heads up to bed early. Her room is in the attic; the space has been cleared out to make it into a room for her. It's still pretty dusty, but there is a window, a bed, clean blankets, and the perfect ledge where, if she hoisted herself through the window using the bed to gain height, she could skid down the tiled roof and watch and wait until the coast was clear. She could shimmy herself along the roof, under the cover of darkness, and make her way to the side of the farmhouse. There she can use the drainpipe to lower herself down to the first floor ledge, recover, and then slowly make it the rest of the way down. So when she is sure no one is about, she does just that, landing lightly on her feet. She pauses and listens and then runs low to the shrubs that cover the base of the exterior wall. She hides in those bushes and waits until the patrol has passed before clambering over the wall — she is almost grateful for the GDO's gruelling training programme, without which she would never have had the upper body strength for the climb.

She drops down the other side and runs in the shadows to the drop point — an abandoned caravan a quarter of a mile down the road. When she reaches it, she crawls underneath and finds the matchbox-sized device taped near the exhaust. She removes it and runs back up the road, over the wall, waits, and then looks up at the drainpipe and thinks better of it. She wipes her face with her sleeve, checks herself for dirt, and sneaks back into the farmhouse and into the kitchen.

"Hey, shrimp, you look kinda clammy, you sick?" Carl asks.

"Nah, it's just hot in the roof and I forgot to keep the window open. Just getting some water." Carl fills up a glass and hands it to her.

"Thanks." She smiles at him and leaves the kitchen, listening carefully to every sound. There are some people in the old living room — Ham, Dune, and Echo by the sounds of it. She pauses by the door to the debriefing room and listens. Not a sound. She turns the handle but it is locked. Dammit, she thinks, she hasn't anything on her to pick the lock with, but then she remembers the chimney... if it is open, she can drop the device down it and just hope no one sees it in the grate the next morning. She climbs the stairs slowly, thinking, and then makes her way back to her room and back out the window. She just has to figure out which chimney stack is the right one.

Rage sets the timer on the device for 45 minutes so that she can have an alibi in case anything goes wrong. She calculates which chimney it *should* be and makes a silent prayer as she drops the device down the stack and goes back through to her room, down the stairs, and back outside and to the mess. There she finds most of the Sault team relaxing and laughing. They welcome her in and she sits down and joins in their fun, and waits.

CASSIA

Rae has fallen asleep on the sofa next to me; her breathing is soft and even.

"I can carry her to her room," Luca suggests. I look at her and think about how she came to find us late at night, looking agitated.

"I think she should be in the barn with us."

"I'll put her in your bed."

I raise my eyebrow at him. "I don't think that the camp beds we're in will hold both of us. Not comfortably anyway."

"So presumptuous! I was going to offer you mine and I'd sleep on the floor or in here." He scoops her small body up into his arms.

Luca carries her carefully and tucks her into my bed. And then I climb into his. "Night, sucker."

He scowls at me. "I'm regretting my plan." He then climbs into the bed with me.

"Luc." I'm trying to control my laughing so as not to wake Rae. "Get off me." There's no space so he's just lying on top of me.

"But I just want to be close to you, Cass." I accidentally let out a snort, which starts him laughing and the little camp bed begins to shake.

"What fresh hell is this?" Yve says as she walks into the room. Luca and I shush her and point to Rae.

"If you two even kiss whilst I'm in the same room I am going to throw a bucket of cold water over you."

"Sorry Yve." I pout at her. Luca then decides to plant sloppy kisses all over my face. "Save me, Yve." Yve climbs on top of Luca's back, licks her palms, and smears them over his face. I'm laughing so hard now that tears are pouring down my cheeks as I'm trying so hard not to make a sound. Luca practically squeals with disgust and manages to climb off me with Yve still on his back.

"If this is how every night goes, I want to start sleeping in here." We all look guiltily across at Rae.

"Sorry to wake you," I whisper unnecessarily.

Jono and Drummer then enter our dorm with mischief written all over them, and I look at Rae apologetically. There's no way she's going to be getting back to sleep for a while.

Finally, everyone falls asleep. Luca sleeps on the floor next to me, with Rae in my bed, but it's not long before we're all woken by Rae's screams. I leap out of bed and nearly trip over Luca. Everyone is up and out of their cots, ready to defend her, but she's having a nightmare. She's still screaming, so I lie down next to her and hold her. The concern for our youngest member makes everyone twitchy. They don't know how to soothe her but they care, I can see it on their faces. So I just hold her until her screams turn to whimpers.

"That's not a normal nightmare," Jono whispers, and we all know what he means — it is the nightmares we've all experienced, one dredged up from a place of experience. What have those soldiers done to her? She's still shaking as I hold her and I don't leave her side until morning.

When she wakes up, I see a flash of anger when she realises she's not alone, but then her expression turns to confusion.

"Why are you here?"

"You had a nightmare. I fell asleep next to you when I was trying to calm you down." I also apologise, feeling awkward, like I've crossed a line. I get out of the small bed quickly and step away from her, uncomfortable.

"Oh, well, thanks for taking care of me." She seems confused, as though she's not quite sure how to process this information, and she can't look at me in the eyes.

"It's no problem, we've all had them."

"You have?" Rae seems disbelieving.

"Except Cassia never gets into bed with any of us, not even Luca." I throw a pillow at Jono for the remark and he pouts.

"Isn't Carl expecting you on kitchen duty 'shrimp'?" Drummer says, as he hauls himself out of bed.

"Oh, yeah he is."

"Can we get extra rations seeing as you're in our team?" Drummer asks.

"I am?" Rae seems more bewildered by this than anything.

"'Course you are," Jono replies, and we all nod in agreement. And then she smiles, and it's a nervous, small thing but for some reason I feel like it's the first genuine one since she arrived.

"In that case, I better get to work." She throws back the covers and runs for the stairs.

"Hey!" Luca calls. "Want us to move your bed in here?"

She turns and nods enthusiastically and then runs down the stairs.

"We need to get the kid more clothes," Yve says behind me. I turn to her. "That sparkly t-shirt is just not going to do."

"Anyone good with a needle? They have spare uniforms in storage."

Jono scratches his head and looks at me sheepishly. "I may be able to sew." We all look at him confused.

"I was really into fancy dress at one point, okay?"

"His costumes were amazing, to be fair," Drummer offered. "He used to make them for me, too, and always insisted on measuring my inside leg." Jono groans and the rest of us laugh.

In the late morning, we're called in to meet with Dune. The devices they found are all duds; they'd somehow been wiped or were already dead, so they can't get anything off them. "However, we do know they're a high-tech communications device — two types by the looks of things. They may be prototypes or they might be already in use. We need to know more. Echo is going to head up your team, and you're going to look into this and bring me anything you can. Tonight you're going to scope out a nearby GDO base and see what you come back with."

And so we began to prepare for our next mission.

RAGE

Rage doesn't want to hang around waiting for the others whilst they are debriefed, and so she makes her way to the barn where she knows the prisoners are being kept. She goes around the side of the barn, half of which is where the supplies are stored, and uses the windowsill as leverage to pull herself to standing. She searches the crumbling brickwork for hand and foot holds, then when she's made sure she has a path to the next ledge she climbs up, marks out her next route, and then scrambles into the rafters through a very security-lax hole in the eaves.

She crawls along a supporting beam whilst looking down, pausing when she hears voices. She looks around at the layout of the attic with its rotten boards, cobwebs, dust, and most likely rats, but none of this bothers her. She is bothered by whether she can find somewhere secure enough and comfortable enough for her to watch and listen to what's happening below. Luck has it that a light is switched on, and she sees the beam shine up through a fissure in the ceiling below. She shunts along, rests her head on the crook of her arm, and peers down.

There is a soldier inside the room, a GDO soldier, head down on a desk, but no one else is in there that she can see. Gently, she pokes her fingers into the crack where the light is coming through, crumbling the old plaster, and watches it fall to the floor in tiny flakes. They fall around him like snow but he doesn't appear to have noticed them. She makes the hole only slightly wider so that she can see better, but not too wide as she doesn't want to be spotted. Then, she waits.

She drifts off for a little while, which is surprising considering she's lying on a sharp-edged wooden beam. She is woken up when she hears footsteps below. One of the things the GDO has taught her is to be a light sleeper, to always be on alert. Like the night before, she'd known they were going to carry her to bed, that Luca had cradled her in his arms. She'd pretended to be asleep through it all, pretended that she was doing that to gain more intel, pretended that it wasn't because she couldn't remember ever feeling so safe.

A man walks into the room below her, one she doesn't remember seeing before. He's wearing a blue button-down shirt tucked into jeans, with black, polished shoes. From where she is positioned, she can see his baldness very clearly. He sits down in the chair opposite the GDO soldier and waits. When the soldier doesn't move, he slams the palm of his hand down onto the table. Slowly the soldier lifts his head.

"I do hope you enjoyed your sleep," said the balding man. The GDO soldier doesn't reply. The balding man slides something across the table — it is one of the Symbio implants. The soldier sits back in his chair.

"Now this was an interesting little find." Rage was panicking. The soldier doesn't know that she's disabled the devices; he's going to play into their hands. "So the GDO has upped their communication game." There's a movement from behind the soldier — she didn't realise another member of the Resistance was in the room, he must have gone into the room when she'd drifted off. He slams the man's head against the table and holds him there as he grunts and bucks. The bald man walks around the table.

"It's incredibly rude to spy on people, you know." The bald man looks behind the soldier's ear and immediately finds the scar that is the mirror image of Rage's. In a surprisingly fast movement, the bald man pulls out a knife and slices behind the GDO soldier's ear. He huffs in pain but doesn't scream; he winces as the bald man pulls out the device, examines it, and frowns.

"Any more? There appear to be two types."

"No, no others." The soldier says. The bald man indicates to the Resistance fighter who then examines the soldier's head, but Rage knows they won't find anything. She and Knight are the only two with Symbio implants. The shipment that the Resistance intercepted must have been for the first batch of recruits to get the implant, which means the GDO are going to start putting more children into the field.

When they realise he doesn't have any more tech on him, they let the GDO soldier sit back up, blood trickling down his neck as he faces his interrogator.

"So you didn't get the upgrade then?" Rage knows that the bald man is guessing, but she has to admit, it is a good bluff.

"It's only just been cleared for use."

"Shame that all those people won't get their new system because of your failure to protect it. I wonder how well the GDO takes such incompetence?"

"You ambushed us! Besides, the tech wasn't for us, it was for those kids they keep like pets."

Rage is even more impressed when the bald man doesn't even blink at that. Her heart rate certainly reacts, though. She is also surprised that they treat their enemies better than the GDO ever treats their own recruits. She doesn't have time to dwell on it, though; this development is bad. Knowing there are child soldiers could put her position in jeopardy. She may have to be extracted. She sends a 'com to base, and the reply comes back to take out the interrogator, a known assassin within the Resistance. Rage doesn't have a problem with killing him, but she does have a problem exposing herself, and she says as much to command. She waits for a response, working out how best to strike, thinking only of what she must do, not of what it would mean to do it. The reply finally comes to remain in cover, but if an order does come through for her to strike, then they expect it to be carried out with as much discretion as possible. She doesn't allow herself to feel relief, because that would mean she knows what is being asked of her is wrong. She crawls away from her perch and makes her way back out from under the roof and down to the ground. She needs to strengthen her cover — she needs to make herself seem invaluable, as if she is completely on their side, otherwise everything might fall apart — and that cannot happen.

Shreya is walking towards the mess and so Rage heads towards her. She's been watching the Sault team, and Shreya seems to be the outsider, the one who needs to prove her worth. Rage will give her that and sure up her own position at the same time.

"What are you guys up to today?" Rage asks in a small voice, a voice that makes it sound like she is lonely and needs comfort, a voice that people can't help but respond to.

"Nothing until later, another late night mission." Shreya smiles at her.

"Can I… I mean, would it be okay if I…" Rage looks down, seeming uncomfortable.

"Want to hang out with me for a while?" Shreya says with false nonchalance.

"If that's okay?"

"Sure it is. I have to do a bit of boring work first though, okay?"

"Can I help?"

"How good are you at maps?"

Rage's face lights up. "My dad used to collect them!"

"No kidding. Well, I'm not that good so maybe you can help me."

Shreya leads Rage into the mess and then rolls out the map she's holding onto the coffee table.

"Why aren't you using a digital one?"

Shreya whispers conspiratorially. "No one can hack us with paper."

"Oh yeah… I didn't think of that." Rage smiles sheepishly. "So, umm, what you looking for?"

"There's a base here." Shreya points at the map. "We're going to survey it but we need to find a good approach point."

Rage frowns at the map. "I... I know that place. I passed it when I was running. That must be where those soldiers came from." Rage frowned and spoke to Knight. *'I need an approach point for GDO location sending you now. One that can't be known on a map so they have to take me along.'*

"Okay, searching now."

"Do you remember anything about it?" Shreya asks, hopefully.

"Umm, I'm trying to remember." Rage takes a deep breath and closes her eyes as Knight sends her a live stream from a soldier on the base.

"Are you okay, you've gone a little green?"

Rage opens her eyes. "Yeah, just don't like to remember." Rage takes in a shaky breath. "There's a small stream that's not on the map, it has a high bank, I hid there for a bit. Does that help?"

"Yeah, it helps! Do you think you can find it on the map?"

Rage examines the map. "No, I can't tell on here. I'm sorry."

"Rae, I know it's scary, but do you think you could come with us and show us where we can watch them from?" Shreya looks incredibly hopeful.

Rage bites her lip and then nods and offers a small smile.

Shreya goes to clear her plan with Dune and leaves Rage alone.

"Could've warned me about the video stream," Rage grumbles.

"Kept your cover even more though, didn't it?" She doesn't like the smugness she is feeling rolling off Knight's words.

"I'm force feeding you custard next time I see you."

"Fine, if you want to be puked on, go right ahead."

CASSIA

I'm annoyed with Shreya for convincing Dune to allow Rae to join our mission. A child her age has no place working on a military recon assignment. I argued with Dune and Echo about it, and Echo backed up Rae, saying she'd be protected and to let her prove her worth, just like the rest of us have been able to cement our position with the group through our actions. Grudgingly, I let it go.

I'm anxious throughout our trek in the dark — how on earth is Rae even going to recognise where she hid that night, especially since at the time she was scared. We walk in silence, which I always think must be hard for Jono and Drummer, but their faces are serious. It's sometimes strange to think of them as soldiers, as Resistance fighters. It feels like it's against their nature, but I suppose, it isn't in Luca's or mine either.

Rae, amazingly, leads us straight to the stream, and she's right, it's the perfect spot to monitor the GDO. I feel bad for not giving her more credit. We all wait in silence and watch the rotations, count the numbers, and then return to base with no problems, no ambushes, no true danger. Back at base, we report back our findings.

The next morning, Dune decides to join our mission that same night, along with Ham, Echo, and fortunately not Ian, who apparently is in charge of the prisoners. The thought gives me shivers; oddly, it makes me feel sorry for the GDO soldiers held hostage.

As we gear up for the night, Dune explains that communication devices were removed from behind the right ear of each of the GDO detainees. It's unnerving to think what information they could have fed back to their commanders; I wonder how long we'll be able to stay in the relative comfort of the farm.

"What does that mean for us?" Yve hoists her pack on as she questions Dune.

"You had them in the back of the truck when you delivered them here, at night, and then we took them straight into confinement… but, they're likely to have GPS, so none of that really matters."

"So they know we're here?" I ask.

"Yes, they know we're here, and the fact that they haven't hit us yet means they're waiting for… something."

"Something, like what?" Shreya looks concerned.

"That I don't know, but we need to be ready… for anything." He looks to Echo who inclines her head in agreement.

We start our two-mile walk and I'm paired with Echo. Fortunately, Rae has stayed behind, no longer needed to show us the location. I'm glad I'm with Echo; I haven't had the chance to really speak with her at all. It'll be good to get to know someone who managed to get so high up within GDO ranks as a spy — maybe there are things we can all learn. Dune certainly relies on her inside knowledge a lot by using her as his second.

We're far enough out at this point that we can still talk, although quietly.

"What do you think the GDO are waiting for?"

She's silent for a moment, then, "I imagine they're waiting to find a way to stop the Resistance for good."

"How would they be doing that?"

Her green eyes are bright in the darkness. "That's what I'm worried about…"

"You don't think…"

"There's a spy? Maybe, it would explain the wait. It would mean they're gathering everything they can before their final strike."

"*Final* strike?"

"We're not as strong as you might think, Cassia."

"I know the GDO are larger than we are, but if we can get the people on our side—"

"No, Cassia, they're stronger, more organised, have money behind them, technology, and they're everywhere." Her tone is patronising and I really don't like it.

"Then why are you fighting at all?" I'm irritated now.

"Why? Because that's what you do when you're oppressed. You fight back, you hold on to hope, otherwise... what's the point?"

"That sounds like something Dune would say."

"It is something Dune said, when he asked me to join his fight."

"I don't want to pry and if you don't want to answer, but... you were betrayed, right?"

She takes in a slow, deep breath. "By my girlfriend. She was my boss and I thought she wanted the same things I did but, well, you never really know people."

The pain in her voice is unmistakable. "I'm sorry, that must have been awful."

She looks away from me and adds, "And then she tortured me."

"Oh, Echo."

She smiles, bitterly. "Nothing strengthens your resolve more than being betrayed and beaten by the woman you love."

"I'm glad you have Dune."

"I suppose nothing gets past you, then?" Her smile is genuine now.

"He's a good man — I don't think he would do anything to hurt you."

"No, I don't think he would. You know, we're lucky, you and I, to find decent people."

I look at Luca up ahead. "Yeah, it makes a big difference knowing that there's someone who will always have your back. I mean, I know we all have each other's backs here, but, you know what I mean."

"Yeah, I know what you mean."

"Has Dune said anything about Rae?" I ask, worried that I won't like the answer.

"He's insistent she gets moved off base."

"Oh, right. Where would she even go?" My heart sinks; I'm not sure whether Rae would be safer with us or a family within a heavily occupied GDO town.

"Exactly, that's why I've insisted she stays." Echo gives me a conspiratorial look, and I smile. I'm starting to feel less intimidated by her.

We're less than a mile away from the GDO base now, so we have to be silent and start to communicate using hand signals. We split up in our pairs so that we can surround the base. Echo and I make our way to the west side of the camp and wait for Dune's signal.

Even though we had instigated a prison break back in Camburg, we haven't yet performed a full raid on a GDO camp. I know the tactics, I know my role, but even so, my stomach is filled with aggressive butterflies, and I feel nauseated.

We get the signal and move forward from our hiding spot in the trees. Echo covers my back as I take the front. She's surprised from the side as we breach the outer perimeter of the base, a gun held to her temple. I turn and whip the butt of my rifle upwards into the soldiers chin, knocking his head back. He goes down.

"Nice shot, squaddie," whispers Echo, winking at me. We keep moving. We approach the first building and I go to the right, Echo to the left. I check my surroundings and before I see or hear it, I sense something, someone. I turn and there's a soldier behind me. I raise my rifle but I'm not fast enough; they bring their right arm up, using their pistol to smack me across the temple. The pain is blinding, and then I black out.

RAGE

As Rage watches the team head out, she sits at the end of her bed in the empty dorm and thinks hard about what she is going to do. Then she thinks about Knight and sends details of the mission to base, and at their request, includes the names of all the Resistance fighters, too. She feels funny about it, like there is something crawling inside her skin. Maybe she just hasn't been active enough that day; she is used to a lot more exercise than she is getting. She heads outside and begins to walk laps of the compound.

Carl joins her after her third lap. "You know, they're going to be okay."

"Yeah, I know that."

He puts his hands into the pockets of his shorts. "It doesn't get easier, watching them go out and risk their lives."

"It's worse when you can't go, when you don't know what's happening."

"Yeah, shrimp, it's definitely harder when you can't be out there."

Rage scowls. "Was it the GDO that did that to you?"

Carl nods and continues. "We were ambushed by them. It was early on in the fight, I was lucky that hospitals were still fully functional back then, otherwise, who knows what would have happened."

"I'm glad you lost your legs when you did, then."

Carl laughs. "Thanks, shrimp."

"Don't call me shrimp anymore," Rage grumbles.

"Why not, shrimp?" he smirks.

"Makes me sound weak." Rage crosses her arms and picks up the pace a little, but it doesn't faze Carl who keeps in step with her.

"Oh, I see. Want to be a soldier like the rest of us?"

"Yeah, I do." And the truth of the sentiment is clear.

"I could train you." Carl scratches at the stubble on his neck whilst looking at Rage through the corner of his eyes.

"Really? How to use a gun?" She stops and beams at him.

"Woah, calm down there, I'm not going to train you to use a gun, but I will teach you how to defend yourself."

"Can we start now?"

"Only if I can keep calling you shrimp, shrimp."

Rage glares at him. "Fine."

"Okay, shrimp, let's get to work."

Carl leads Rage towards the lawn and then turns to face her. He teaches her how to get out of a chokehold, how to block a knife attack, and how to disarm someone; they are all things she already knows, but she wants the practice and puts up a good show of not knowing what she's doing. Had she been a novice, Carl would be a good teacher. He is patient and clear with his instructions, hugely different to how she'd been trained when she was taken by the GDO.

As Rage walks back to the mess to shower, she remembers how the GDO had taught her lessons.

The second time she had ran away, she had made it as far as the closest village. She was nine years old. She'd worried about leaving Knight but had decided the only way to keep him safe was for her to go and find some help. There must be someone outside, a policeman or something, someone who could save them.

When they caught her they didn't beat her; the things they did to her then were much worse, much more permanent, and the buzzing and grinding of the saw was the only warning she'd ever get that they were about to start. It was the signal. Saw switched on, metal tray laid out in front of her with all the implements neatly lined up and sterilised. Straps tightened. Faintly she remembers a time long before when she'd sat in a similar chair with sterilised implements laid out before her, and when the chair was tipped back and her mouth was opened for inspection there was a poster of a hippo having his teeth inspected by an elephant stuck to the ceiling. There were no posters on the ceiling in the room she was held in by the GDO, only track marks of old, dried-out leaks.

They never used the saw, the one that would take fingers. They always threatened to take her fingers. She wonders if they had actually used it on her, whether she would have stopped fearing it. Maybe that's why they never did. They taunted her with it, built up her dread of it.

This is what will happen, this is what will happen, this is what will happen.

And she'd play the moment the saw buzzed through her bones, and the blood, and the pain, and it kept playing over and over and over.

The memory throbs through her as Rage showers. She holds her arms and shivers, even though the water is warm, and in her mind the saw's buzzing keeps playing, over and over and over.

***

She's still shivering when the team returns from their raid. She runs to the farmhouse to see them come in and instantly she knows something's wrong.

"What happened?"

"It was a trap," Dune says, and throws down his pack and kicks a chair so that it skids across the dining room floor.

Luca storms out of the room, and Rage watches him go with shock and then looks around at the injured team. Cassia isn't there.

"Where's Cass?" she asks, her voice higher than normal. Drummer looks at the others and then sits down in a chair opposite where Rage is standing.

"Rae, she was taken from us."

"Ta— what do you mean? She's d-dead?" she stammers, alarmed. Has she got Cassia killed?

"No, captured."

"Captured? But why?"

Drummer looks at Dune who is standing with his arms crossed, seething. "We think it may have something to do with an old enemy from our time in Auria. He is the only reason I can think they'd take only her." Dune bites out the words. "Why didn't I see this? We knew that they were waiting for something. It doesn't surprise me that that man would target her."

"But why would he target Cassia?" Rage asks, confused. Genuinely confused, as this wasn't specified in her mission. Cassia was never mentioned by name, only the Resistance camp as a whole. What wasn't she being told?

"Because, although she may look like any old eighteen year old, she managed to humiliate and beat him, because she's magnificent." Yve was proud as she spoke, but tears glistened in her eyes. "Just know, kid, she's so much stronger than she looks, and she never, ever gives up."

Rage looks around the room, wide-eyed. "What's he going to do with her?" No one could answer.

Rage leaves the team and goes to sit up in the attic, even though it is no longer her room since she'd been made an honorary member of Sault.

"Knight?"

"Rae? What is it? What's happened?" He sounds panicked, and she can almost feel his heart beating faster.

"I... I did something bad."

"Tell me." His voice is calm, the same voice that saves her from the silences, from the darkness in her own mind.

"I told command about a raid and they've taken one of the team hostage. She — she's sort of nice to me." Rage realises her hands are shaking; she isn't sure what this means.

"I'll see what I can find out."

"Knight, I didn't know they were going to take her." He can tell she's desperate for him to believe her.

"I know." Because he does know, even if she doesn't know it herself.

"If I didn't —"

"I know." Knight pauses. *"When you come back, we should go swimming."*

"Swimming…? Where?"

"In our pool, of course. I've bought us floats."

"Oh? What kind of floats?"

"One's a giant pizza slice."

"A pizza slice?" She smiles despite her shame — this is a game they have often played, where they pretend they are living a different life.

"And a swan for me."

Rage snorts. *"I'd rather have a shark."*

"Fine, a shark for you." His smile warms her insides.

"I miss you, Knight."

"I miss you too, Rae."

Rage is making her way back towards the dorms hoping to find Luca, when she sees him sitting in the apple orchard, which runs alongside the storage and prison barn.

She sits down next to Luca and doesn't say a word. He looks off down through the rows of fruit trees and into the night beyond. They sit there in silence for a long time before Luca speaks. "I didn't realise they had taken her until it was too late." Rage waits. "When we entered the buildings they were empty, we only encountered a few soldiers who fled rather than fought. We knew that it was odd, that it meant something, but I didn't check on her, I should have checked she was okay."

"How were you supposed to know that she was going to be taken?"

"I should have known Kohler wouldn't let it rest, that he'd seek his revenge."

"Because you all humiliated him?"

"Yes, and because…" Luca looks at Rage for the first time. "He's a dangerous man, and now that he has her…"

"Yve says she's strong, even though she doesn't look it."

"She is strong, she was the spark of the rebellion in Auria."

"Cassia was?"

"Has no one told you?" Rage shakes her head. Through his misery, Luca's face still fills with pride as he speaks. "She wanted to free her father from prison and so she joined the GDO as a soldier and I joined up with her. I suppose I was her first recruit. Then she got Drummer and Jono to join, and well, let's just say she brought us all together, gave us a purpose."

"Well, in that case she will definitely be okay."

"If it wasn't Kohler I would have some hope, but Rae, you're too young to know, to have seen what we've seen. The world isn't a kind place and it definitely became a lot worse once the GDO took over." But she did know, maybe more than he did.

"So we've gotta get her back then."

Luca looks at the small girl next to him and smiles. "Yes, yes we do."

Rage gives a sharp nod and then stands up, holding her hand out to Luca. "We've got work to do."

WEEK TWENTY-FOUR

CASSIA

I awake to the most blinding agony I've ever experienced. I'm lying on my side and the room swims when I open my eyes. I retch and then vomit bile over the bed and floor. That's when I realise I'm in a bed, but it's not my bed in the farm — the sheets are white, crisp linen, the likes of which I haven't seen in so long. It feels a shame to have spoilt them with my sick. I try to think but I can't piece anything together — the back of my neck burns, my temple throbs, and the room keeps spinning until I tumble back into blackness.

WEEK TWENTY-FIVE

RAGE

Rage has been up most of the night, trying to brainstorm with Clive — over a secure channel — how to track down Cassia. Knight is now asleep — he had found no trace of Cassia in the GDO system, and he'd been trying for days. Kohler is hiding Cassia and hiding her well.

Rage puts down the tablet and rubs her eyes. She's sitting in the empty kitchen, playing with a stray piece of onion skin, when Echo walks in.

"What are you still doing up?" Echo goes to the sink and gets herself a glass of water, and then sits down opposite Rage.

"Speaking to Clive."

"You guys get anywhere?"

Rage runs her hands through her short hair and realises that it's greasy — when did she last wash it? She can't remember. "No, nowhere. Wherever she is, it's not on the GDO's radar."

"I hate to say it, but this Kohler guy is smart — he knew we'd try and find her and so hid her where even his own people couldn't track her." Echo thinks for a moment and then leans forward. "How do you feel about hot chocolate?"

"Like it's something I haven't had since before." Rage says absently.

"Well, I may have something stashed away." Echo goes to one of the kitchen cupboards and rummages around at the back, pulling out a tub of chocolate powder. She grins conspiratorially at Rage and puts a pan of milk onto the stove.

"How chocolatey do you like it?" Rage shrugs and goes over to the hob and leans over the pan, marvelling as Echo stirs in the chocolate powder.

"This reminds me of my mum." Rage says unexpectedly. She hadn't meant to say that, hadn't even realised she was thinking it. She made a point of not thinking about her, about her life before. But now, she can picture her, her black hair cropped much like hers is now, tucked behind her ears as she stirs a pan of hot chocolate in their tiny kitchen. Small gold studs in the shape of leaves catch the light, earrings she wore every day. Her brown eyes wrinkle with a smile as she sees Rage watching in anticipation of her treat — a bowl of hot chocolate. She sprinkles a pinch of cinnamon into the pan, a dash of vanilla. Then, out of the fridge, she pulls out a bowl of whipped cream and spoons some on top of Rage's bowl, passing it to her and kissing her on the forehead. What does she say to her then? Rage tries to remember but she can't. The memory feels like it's slipping away from her. Everything is hazier around the edges than before. Is it possible to forget a parent completely? She's almost completely forgotten her father, but he died so long ago it's not surprising. She realises with horrifying clarity that her mother will slip away from her in much the same way. And then who will she be? Not even an orphan — a daughter of war.

Echo hands her a mug of hot chocolate with a gentle smile, and Rage slams closed her thoughts. It will do her no good to think about before.

"You know, before all of this…" Echo waves her hand around, indicating the war, "I wasn't anybody. I was at university, finishing up my final year studying history. I was going to go travelling, see the world." Her smile is sad. "I've seen far more of human nature in this war than I would have seen getting drunk on a beach in Thailand." She sips her drink. "Sometimes I wonder if it's a good lesson to learn young, that if you're not careful, the darkness that lurks within us all can become corrupting."

"You know I'm just a kid, right?" Rage says, even though she understands Echo perfectly.

"I wish you were just a kid. If you were then I wouldn't have seen some of the worst things man is capable of."

"Do you think we can win this war?"

Echo doesn't answer right away like any of the others would — they'd be certain, hopeful. Instead, she considers the question. "I honestly don't know, kid, but you have to fight for what you believe in, otherwise, what's the point?"

And Rage understands exactly what Echo means. She hadn't fought for what she believed in until Cassia was captured. Even though she is scared, it feels *true* to be trying to get her back. She doesn't get that uncomfortable feeling in her stomach, like when she revealed Resistance plans to the GDO.

"If we win, what will you do? Travel the world?" Rage asks.

"I think I'd like to rest, live somewhere rural with someone I want to spend my life with — try and track down missing friends and family. I don't have the desire to travel any more. I've seen more than enough."

"Do you think the rest of the world is like Old Europe?"

"It's not how it was when I was young, that's for sure. Things just seemed to fall apart, almost overnight. You never see trouble coming until it's too late. The historians will see the warnings, say how blind we were."

For the first time in a long time, Rage feels helpless. She's taken back control of her life in some small way, but now, with Cassia gone, she feels adrift.

The next morning, Echo joins Sault team as they discuss plans to find Cassia. — bases to attack, land to scope out. And Rage allows herself to hope once again that they will find her friend, but she knows something will have to change, because despite everything she is trying to protect, spying for the GDO feels very, very wrong now.

Shreya sits down next to Rage and gives her a gentle elbow. "You know what? Cassia's stubborn as hell. She won't let anything bad happen, simply to spite the GDO."

"Is that why you two don't get on?" Rage asks.

Shreya is shocked by Rage's perceptiveness. "We disagree about something that happened, that's all. Doesn't mean I don't respect her and all that she's done."

"Grudgingly," Rage adds.

Shreya smiles and then laughs. "Something like that."

"Can I join Sault team tonight?"

"Like I said, Cassia's stubborn and she would kill every single one of Sault team, even Luca, if she got back and found out we'd dragged you out on another mission."

"Fine," Rage says grumpily.

Rage waits in the mess for Sault team to return. When they finally come back, just before dawn, she's asleep on the sofa. A muddy Jono wakes her gently.

"No luck this time, kid," he says, the strain evident on his face. Drummer collapses onto the sofa next to Rage.

"We'll find her, though." Drummer musters enough conviction to almost sound as though he believes his own lie.

"Dune wants us to stop looking, we're getting too distracted from the main mission." Rage's voice is quiet as she confesses the information.

"How'd you know that?" Jono asks.

Rage shrugs. "Might've been listening at a keyhole."

Drummer's head falls back against the sofa. "She wouldn't stop looking for us." He takes a breath. "Luca's going to lose it."

"Do you think he has it in him to get really mad?" Jono questions.

"Mad like, really quiet and broody... in a sexy way." Some of Drummer's usual humour comes through as he speaks.

"I wouldn't let Pranav hear you saying things like that, you naughty boy," Jono teases. Rage falls quiet and listens as Jono and Drummer talk with good humour, and wonders what it'll mean for Cassia if they can't save her.

The next morning Dune tells Sault team that they can no longer spend their time searching for Cassia, that they will keep the team apprised of any chatter that might signify where she is, but until that time, they need to start working on Resistance missions again.

Cassia was lost to them.

WEEK TWENTY-SIX

CASSIA

The next time I wake up I'm still in agony and I'm sluggish and dizzy, but I am able to look around. I'm in a room by myself, something I haven't had the luxury of since living with Luca's family in my tiny room under the stairs. There's a drip attached to my left arm, the pain in my neck is now just a pinch, and my temple no longer throbs, but my head still aches in a way I've never experienced before and I can't stop feeling seasick.

I sleep on and off for a while, fitfully. I'm having nightmares still, but they're different now, and I can't quite keep hold of them when I wake up. The panic I feel as I wake tells me that these are the worst yet, and that maybe my mind is forgetting them on purpose.

Eventually I'm visited by a doctor who won't answer my questions but examines me. And then I'm left alone again, wondering what they want of me. The doctor had injected something into my cannula and soon the world turns hazy, and I fall into a deep, deep sleep.

I wake up in dirt. There is nothing more confusing than first waking up in a strange bed and then waking up in cold damp earth. My head feels a little clearer — I push myself up off the ground and look around. It's dawn, and in the near distance I can see the farmhouse. I look around in shock — why would I have been dropped back here? What does it mean?

I walk unsteadily up the lane, the sentry pointing his gun at me as I approach, and then he recognises me. It's Jono.

"Cass?! *Cass?!*" I half collapse and he catches me, and then helps me inside. I sit down on the bench at the rustic table in the large kitchen; Carl practically collapses down next to me when he sees me.

"You're... here? You're alive?"

"It doesn't feel like it." I hold my head in my hands and Jono runs off somewhere. There's shouting and then the pounding of feet. I hear a skid and then down on his knees before me is Luca, my Luca.

"We've been searching everywhere for you." There are tears in his eyes. Have I ever seen tears in his eyes? I don't remember, and everything is getting blurry... I fall into his arms, unconscious.

When I wake up next the smell of mud has gone from my nostrils — I'm clean and in one of the rooms in the farmhouse. Luca is beside me.

He strokes my hair back from my face. "How do you feel?"

"Strange, but better than I was." My throat is so dry that it hurts to talk. Luca holds a glass of water out for me and I sit up and sip it slowly.

"What happened?"

"I don't know. I was in a hospital, or something. There was a doctor. And then I woke up in the mud." I frown; I can't think, can't focus through the vapour in my brain.

"Why did they bring you back?"

I look at him but nothing. I have nothing.

"It's okay, don't worry about that, just rest. I'm so happy to have you back." And he kisses my forehead, my temple, my cheek, the back of my hand, my palm. And I fall back to sleep feeling safe in a way that I can only feel when I'm with him.

The next time I come around I feel more like myself, the effects of whatever drug they gave me having worn off and the ache in my head finally receded into the background. Luca is still in the room with me, and Rage is asleep in the corner on an armchair, curled up like a cat.

Luca sees me looking at her. "She's been worried about you. Insisted on coming on recces, but we didn't let her," he quickly reassures me. "Basically leading the troops. She's a leader that small one."

"You look tired; you need to sleep too." My voice is hoarse.

"I can't, I've tried." I pull myself up to sitting and then step out of the bed.

"I'll be back in a minute." I carefully make my way to the bathroom and close the door, not locking it as per Luca's instructions in case I collapse. As I'm washing my hands there's a strange ringing in my ears, almost like a PA system getting feedback. I grip the porcelain beneath my hands and then a voice sounds in my head and I swear I'm going mad. That can be the only explanation, because it's Captain Kohler's voice.

"Hello, Fortis." I retch but my stomach is empty. *"Do you like your surprise?"*

"What surprise?" I think, and he answers me, oh God, he *answers* me.

"The Symbio technology, the one that I implanted the day I realised I could get to you. I've been waiting for yours to take, for this moment."

"Get out of my head!"

"There's no escape from us, Fortis. This is the end for you, for all of you. I just wanted to do you the curtesy of letting you know first."

"Get out!" I scream inside my head, and then I'm screaming out loud without realising it.

"GET OUT GET OUT GET OUT GET OUT!"

Luca comes storming into the bathroom. "What is it? What's happening?"

I'm crouched on the floor holding my head and screaming, screaming, screaming. My tormentor has somehow managed to enter my mind. I feel violated, my skin crawls, and my stomach roils.

"He's in my head," I manage to gasp.

"Who?"

I'm shaking uncontrollably and Luca is holding me. I notice in the doorway Rae is standing there looking shocked and unsure, and I can hear more people coming.

"Kohler, he's in my head."

"Did you miss me, little Cassia?"

"Leave me ALONE."

"Never, not until this is done, not until I have what is mine."

"No."

"I will have you, I will crush all of you."

I'm pulling at my hair now, and Luca has to hold onto my hands because I'm starting to rip strands from their roots. I am tormented. I am possessed.

Dune strides into the bathroom, "What's going on?"

"She says Kohler is in her head?" Luca looks up at him questioningly.

"A device? Behind her ear?"

"I checked that when she first got back."

Rae backs away from the door, scared out of her wits, confused by what's happening. I don't want to scare her, I really don't, but it's *him. Inside. My. Head.*

"He must have put one on her somewhere." Luca ever so gently starts to check me, but I get frustrated with him; he needs to find it and NOW. "It'll be sore; they only implanted it two weeks ago."

"My neck!"

Luca brushes my hair forward and draws in a breath. "There's a fresh scar."

I suck in a deep breath.

"Get it out, please get it out." I'm crying now, and I want to claw my skin open but Luca's holding my hands.

"Shit, doc got called out to the field... I'll get Ian," Yve says. I didn't know she was in here. I don't even feel nervous that Ian's going to cut it out; I just want it torn from my body as quickly as possible.

"Oh, and Fortis?" I don't respond; I can't bear to respond. *"You're mine."* I'm sobbing so hard and I'm trying to pull my hands out of Luca's grip but he won't let me, won't let me hurt myself, but I have to. Why doesn't he understand? I have to. I have to get that man out of my head.

Ian rushes into the bathroom, sweaty, a knife in hand and a bottle of vodka.

"Rest her head over the bath."

Ian's hands are soft and warm, not clammy and cold like I'd imagined. He rinses the knife in the spirit before he approaches me. He's gentle with me; I feel kindness in his touch, which I hadn't expected. We only have anaesthetic for emergencies and so I know that he's going to have to slice into my skin and pull out the device without any painkillers.

He's so quick and sure with the knife that I don't feel it when he cuts, but I do feel the knife pushed into my flesh to pull out the device. I scream. Through my howling I hear him saying there are wires and Luca tells him to cut them, feeling my panic, but Dune is worried what cutting them will do to me

"Do it!" I scream, but he doesn't. "Just pull it out," I moan.

"We don't know how it's implanted, what it could do to you." Dune is trying to be consoling but I can't be consoled.

"Just do it. Please." I can't stop crying — from the pain, from the defilement, from the return of all my fears.

"No! Stop!" It's Rae.

"Rae, it's okay, I'm okay, they're just going to pull it out. The worst is over."

"No, if you pull it out wrong she might die!"

"Rae, it's okay, it's okay." And Ian steps back and I'm furious at Rae for speaking up, for stopping them from tearing this parasite from me.

"I'm not doing it; it's somehow connected to her brain. She needs a surgeon."

Yve comes in carrying a med kit and offers to be the one to sew me up. A gesture of friendship that not many could offer. She's as gentle as she can be, but without anaesthetic, it's excruciating.

They give me the room in the farmhouse for an extra night, big enough for Luca to lie next to me. For now, Kohler is quiet, but I know he's there, in my head. I might never escape him.

The demons from my nightmares are real and I am trapped, indefinitely, in true hell.

RAGE

Rage had done everything she could to try to help retrieve Cassia without giving herself away. She doesn't really understand why this man Kohler wants Cassia, but she knows of the cruelties of the GDO. But even with Knight's help and her own knowledge of the oppressor, they hadn't been able to find Cassia. Rage was the GDO's operative, but whatever they had wanted with Cassia had been off the books, and Rage wonders what that means. Maybe there are a lot of things she doesn't know. She understands there are things above her clearance level, and even though she knows that the atrocities they have committed to the children under their protection are terrible, she's never really thought about what else they might be doing. Her scope has been too small.

"Knight, do you know how to get the Symbio implant out?" Rage asks as she chews on her fingernails, thinking.

"I've been looking, but I'm having to work around the clearance level. What did they do to her?"

"Someone called Kohler has linked to her. They say he did something to her and now he's in her head tormenting her. Who is he?"

She can feel Knight's surprise. *"Our new Major, he's been running your missions."*

"He's command?"

"Yes." Rage's stomach churns — the person she's been feeding information to has harmed Cassia.

"I helped him do this to her."

"So let's do something about it."

"I can't, you know I can't."

"I'm not afraid."

And for the first time in years, Rage feels like she might cry real tears.

"I can't, I can't do it. They'll, they'll…"

Rage can feel Knight's excitement rising. He's been waiting for an opportunity, a reason strong enough to persuade Rage to work against the GDO. *"We just have to be smarter. Feed them false intel. How would they know? They're counting on you to give them what they need to destroy the camp, who, I think, sound like the people whose side we should be on anyway."*

"That doesn't matter."

"Yeah, it does. We know the GDO are bad people."

"But what if—"

"We can't keep helping them, I don't want to help the men who… who…"

"I'm sorry, I'm sorry, Knight. I'll do what I can but I need to be really careful."

"I'll help."

"No, stay out of it, I don't want them to know you're involved."

"But—"

"No, I mean it. If I worry any more about you I won't do it, I'll destroy the whole Resistance camp to keep you safe. Got it?"

"Okay, Rae, I won't do anything." But she's worried that he will. The good thing is she can keep an eye on him, so to speak.

Rage makes her way down from the attic and peeks in through the ajar door to where Cassia and Luca are sleeping. He's curled around her, protecting her, but this isn't an enemy he can keep her safe from. It's up to Rage to find out how to get the implant out. She heads down to the mess to find Yve and discovers that the rest of Sault team are in there, too.

"What did the doc say?" Rage sits down next to Yve.

"Too much of a risk for him to do it, we need a neurosurgeon," Yve replies whilst rubbing her temples, clearly trying to think of what to do.

"Has anyone contacted Clive this morning?" Rage asks the room, and they all look a bit guilty. Rage can't believe that she has to be the one to do everything. She picks up the tablet and enters the dark site login page where she can access a communication link to Clive. "We've got plenty of dead devices but we don't know how they're implanted," she tells them. "I'm gonna ask Clive to see if he can find something, some kind of blueprint or, I dunno, instruction manual for surgeons, so that we can find out how to remove this thing safely."

"And ask him to find a surgeon, still alive and loyal to the Resistance." Shreya leans forward as she speaks, a surprising amount of concern in her tone. Maybe she doesn't hate Cassia after all.

Clive responds rapidly, saying he'll work quickly to get what they need. Rage sits back and looks at the team. "Well, what are you gonna do now?"

"What do you mean, kid?" Yve asks.

"The GDO are planning on taking this base of operation down. Don't we need to plan to stop them? Don't we need to move? Do something?"

"Dune'll handle it," Shreya utters quietly.

"You can't just expect him to handle this all on his own — we need to think of something."

"Kid's got a point. It's not like us to sit around and wait for the bastards to come to us." Yve leans back and crosses her arms, scowling.

"They knew too much about our movements, ever since that night we captured the soldiers."

"They had implants, but they were behind their ears. Pranav looked at them and said they seemed to be more like a mobile phone implant, but the other one, the one Cass has... he said it was fully immersive — it connects into someone else's mind." Drummer unconsciously rubs the back of his neck as he explains.

"What does that mean?" Rage asks, even though she knows all too well what Symbio is and that to her it was a gift as well as a curse.

"That he has unfiltered access to her mind, unlike the 'com link, which works more like a messaging service, where they have control over information that's sent." Yve glares at Drummer.

"He can... he can just go into her mind, access whatever he likes?" She pales.

"Theoretically, if he wanted to."

"Even memories?" Yve asks Drummer.

"I don't know. I think it's just immediate thoughts. He's just speculating."

They are correct; you can't access memories, only immediate thought, but sometimes Rage and Knight's dreams cross over, and their nightmares.

"But if he can do that to her, she can do it to him too, right?" Rage enquires.

"Yes, but kid, I don't know if she's strong enough for that." Yve sounds weary as she speaks.

Rage glares at Yve, letting her childlike persona slip. "You told me she was strong, that despite her appearance she was a leader, that nothing could defeat her. That she would fight, no matter what."

Her heartbeat has doubled. What if Cassia really couldn't get through this?

"I know, Rae, but this is different. He wants her in a very horrible way."

"Just because I'm young doesn't mean I don't know what you mean. She's going to fight back — I know she will." Rage storms out of the mess and goes back into the farmhouse, sits outside the room where Cassia and Luca are sleeping. As soon as Cassia's awake, they're going to get to work because she will not allow her friend to be hurt in this way because of what she did. They would turn this around, they *had* to turn this around; otherwise, she is the worst enemy Cassia has ever encountered. She is no better than the GDO.

CASSIA

"Wake up, Cassia." I focus on trying to block him out. *"That's not going to work, nothing you do will keep me out. I see you tried to remove the device but thought better of it. Wise decision. You'd have been rendered brain dead, which would have been such a shame because the games are just beginning."*

I squeeze my eyes tighter shut and try to think.

"I can hear your thoughts; you're throwing them at me, Fortis. You're not even trying. I have work to do but I'll be back later to check in on you." I can even hear him laughing.

Taking a deep breath, I get out of bed and open the door to find Rae curled in a ball in front of the door. I crouch down beside her and gently tuck her hair behind her ear to wake her. That's when I see it, the faint, old scar behind her right ear — I wouldn't have noticed it but I'm so close it's hard to miss. I freeze — what does this mean? Was it our Rae who betrayed me, who did this to me? I stand and step back in shock. I'm frozen; I don't know how to process this. But then my anger comes.

"Wake up," I whisper harshly into her ear. Her eyes fly open.

"Cass! What's wrong?" I hoist her up to her feet and march her up the stairs into the attic.

"Talk."

"About what?"

I grip her face in my hands and force her head to the side. "About this." Her big blue eyes go wide.

"I... I..."

"Don't lie to me," I glower at her.

Her face hardens into an expression that makes her unrecognisable, and she lifts her chin, "I was sent here to uncover information."

"And you told them about the raid?" I don't break eye contact with her.

"Yes, and they asked for names of every operative going. But, I didn't know about this Kohler, I swear I didn't. When I left he didn't work at the base. Knight said he joined them after I left and has been in command of the mission since then."

"How long have you worked for them?"

"Since I was about six." This shocks me out of my fury.

"*Six?* How?"

She doesn't want to tell me and usually I'd respect that it's too painful to talk about, but she's working for the enemy and I need to know. She must realise this because she begins to talk. "It was just me and my mum. Dad was killed in a car accident years before — I don't remember him. I don't remember it that well." She looks up at me and I'm sorry for her pain but I don't tell her to stop. "The GDO had just come to our town, there were riots on the same day my mum took me to the doctor for a cough, and we came out, and I don't know what had happened, but soldiers were there and they started yelling, and I don't know why, but they…" She takes a breath. "… shot her and left me."

"They didn't take you then?"

"No, I ran to the doctor to help but he locked his door, saying there was nothing he could do. The streets had, by that time, filled with people. I had to fight my way back to her body. Somehow, I got back. I stayed there with her and then two days later they took me."

"You stayed with her for two days?" I sit down on an old trunk.

"I didn't want her to be alone." Her tone is fierce, asking me to challenge her on this.

"Oh, Rae." And like that, my anger has evaporated. "Is that your real name, Rae?"

"It's Rage, only Knight calls me Rae."

"Rage? Why Rage?" I wonder if it's a code name, like Dune and Echo.

When we arrived at the compound we were all numbered, and then, when you finally pass training they let you name yourself. Ever since the day when they shot my mum, I've had these lines of a poem I once heard stuck in my head: *Rage Rage Rage, Until the Mountain Falls Down, Rage Rage Rage, Until the Mountain Falls Down.* I don't remember the rest but I remember the rage part, and that's how I felt." She's embarrassed now. I know the poem — it's famous. She recites it slightly wrong, but I don't correct her.

"It's a good name." She smiles a little at that. "And Night?"

"My best friend, he's my Symbio link."

"Symbio?" I ask.

Rage taps the back of her neck.

"You have it, too?" I stand up and walk behind her, and brush aside her glossy black hair. This scar isn't as faint as the one behind her ear — it's newer. "When?"

"About two years ago. We were their test subjects." She takes a deep breath and then continues, "The tech we have — Symbio — they can't listen in on, which they realised too late. It was a big oversight." I run my finger down her scar absently and she shivers. "But I also have even newer tech."

"More?"

"My eyes."

I look into her dark blue eyes and realise for the first time how unnatural the colour is. "What are they?"

"Implants. They're like contacts you can't remove."

"So they can see what you can see?"

"No, they're still developing it, I can just take photos." I step back, horrified by the idea of the way they've violated her and the lengths they have gone to, to spy on us.

"So you've been with the GDO for six or seven years?" She nods in response. "And you're experienced enough to go undercover?"

"I'm their best operative, one of the first in the youth recruitment programme." She sounds almost proud. "And the first to get to trial tech." She sounds less proud now; I can't imagine the fear of being experimented on. The pain from one implant was bad enough for me. She looks down shyly. "But they taught me stuff, too... Ummm, like, you know that bomb at the petrol station? I built it."

"You did that? To yourself?" I remember her lying there against the rubble, bleeding and broken.

Rage shrugs. I think she was trying to impress me and my reaction has put her out a little. "They were my orders."

"Were you going to tell me, tell us?" And honestly, I think I care more whether or not she was going to tell me.

Rage turns sheepish. "No... but after I found out about them taking you, I haven't given them any information, just the odd thing to keep them off my back, nothing major I swear, and Knight and I decided to help you."

"Night is going to help us?"

"He wanted to all along... I... I was the one who stopped him."

"Why?" She doesn't answer me but I can guess the reason why — she's scared and I don't blame her. "How many more children are there?"

"Hundreds."

"Hundreds?" She doesn't need to say anything for me to know it's true, and I understand her choice in name because I'm experiencing a rage so deep and raw I feel like I might erupt with it. I sit back down and try to think. "This tech — how much can he access?"

"Everything you're thinking, but it's not a constant stream, you have to open up the connection, otherwise you'd be bugged by the other person's internal monologue and wouldn't be able to think."

"How can I tell when he's listening in?"

"It can never be completely a one-way listening device. I always know when Knight is listening to me because his thoughts start to filter in through the connection."

"So if he's spying on me, I'll know about it and be able to think about something innocuous, like, apple picking?"

"I guess so — Knight and I can test it out for you."

"Could you do it now?"

She goes quiet and I wait. It's strange to think she's talking to someone at that moment. She focuses on my face again after about ten minutes of what I assume is experimenting.

"You can override what they hear with inane chatter but you have to be careful because you can easily slip up and think what you're trying so desperately not to think about. Does that make sense?"

"Ish."

She cocks her head to one side and looks through the dirty old skylight thoughtfully before she begins to try to explain. "It's like there are layers of thought. You can fill the space with random unimportant thoughts, but because you're trying so hard not to think of something your subconscious is kinda saying, in the background, what it is you're trying not to say."

"Okay." I rub my face with my hands. "Urgh, this means I can't help plan or be involved with anything." I pause and then look up. "Or…" Rage looks excited, knowing I have an idea. "Can I trust you Rage? Will you work for us? For the Resistance?" I talk to her as a soldier now, knowing that she is older than she seems, that this is her fight, too, for what they have done to her, to Night, and to all those children she's grown up with. "We're going to have two plans, one for me to hide from Kohler and one for Sault to plan without me."

"Yve said you were smart and tough." She pauses and I wonder what she's going to say, then quietly she adds, "I knew she was right."

Now all I have to do is tell the others that I've found our traitor and she's twelve years old.

I ask Rage to wait in the attic whilst I begin telling people about her. I can tell she's nervous and I don't blame her. I'd be nervous, too, especially seeing that if I'm not careful I could accidentally reveal her treachery to Kohler. I go to Luca first, who is awake and finishing getting dressed.

"I was just coming to find you. Where've you been? Everything okay?"

I sit him down and tell him everything Rage has told me. I can see he's angry at first, but I know that's for me, not aimed at her. Luca is a guardian, and he soon becomes concerned for her, as I knew he would.

"Do you think the others will accept her now?" I ask.

"Our team? They accept Jono and Drummer." He says this with a smile.

I surprise myself by chuckling, "That's true."

Luca waits for me to get ready and then walks with me to the barracks. The team is only just getting up. I sit down on Yve's bed, still feeling a little weak and dizzy, and I begin to tell them about Rage.

"She betrayed us and you expect us to trust her now?" Yve says. "I like the kid and I don't wish her harm, but to let her in on our plans… Is that a good idea?"

"She knows them better than we ever will — she could help us turn this fight to our favour. Besides, you and Jake weren't exactly on our side at first, but we trusted each other then…" I really don't want to say any more to open up that wound. "The only harm she's caused is to me, and I'm willing to forgive her that because I honestly believe she didn't know their plan or anything about Kohler. She's a child soldier, what do you think you'd have done at her age in the same situation?" I look around at my friends and wait.

"I always liked the squirt, and Rage is a cool name," Jono states with a smile, affirming his support.

"And you say she can make bombs?" Drummer seems unnervingly excited.

"Apparently it's her speciality."

"We'd be idiots not to work with her," he proclaims.

"If you trust her, I trust her." I'm surprised by Shreya's response but I accept it gladly.

"Hell, I was always going to be in," Yve says, and throws back the covers to reveal she slept in a tank top and knickers. Jono's jaw falls open. "Let's go see the kid and officially enter her into our ranks."

"How do you propose to do that?" Luca's tone is suspicious.

"Well, she has to receive some kind of punishment for her little stunt... I'm sure Jono and Drummer can help me come up with something... unpleasant."

"Just... don't hurt her, okay?" I lament.

"Wouldn't dream of it." Yve grins wickedly.

"Do we tell everyone else?" Drummer says. "Because, I don't know if they'll be as understanding of her as we are." We all go silent at that. It's a good point. By keeping everyone in the dark, we're creating a divide amongst our army, but by letting them in on the secret, they may choose to punish her.

"Maybe once we can prove she's working for us we can let them know," Luca says, and we all agree it's a good plan. We'll keep her secret, for now.

WEEK TWENTY-SEVEN

KOHLER

Major Kohler couldn't quite hide the smile on his face after achieving the first step in his victory, even when the recruits couldn't complete their drills properly. He accepted their failure, for that moment, and permitted them to spend a few hours watching GDO propaganda videos from the early days of their war in Old Europe. He made his way to the underground space where the trainees who weren't fit for active duty worked at computer terminals, inputting predesigned code if they were not intelligent, designing it if they were. Sadly, they have very few designers. He surveyed the room, avoiding entering it unless he had to, and in that moment, he was only interested in one of them. He'd been surprised how robotic they all looked down in the fluorescently lit room. He called out for the recruit he was looking for and the boy stood — he was puny, even punier than most of the outcasts down here. Kohler motioned for him to follow him to his office, and the boy obeyed.

"Night, is that your designated name?"

The boy nodded but didn't speak.

"Mutism."

He nodded again. Kohler held back his irritation — speaking through 'coms was slow and inefficient; he had to wait for the boy to mentally type out his response and then accept each one that was sent through.

"Okay, well, I'm going to need you to respond on 'coms."

"Yes, sir."

"Rage is your Symbio partner, is she not?"

"Yes, sir."

"As you are the first and we're only just installing upgrades on soldiers, I'd like to know — can you access memories?"

"No, sir."

"Nothing?"

"No, sir." Kohler was irritated by this. He observed how the boy's face remained impassive as if everything about him had been muted, not only his voice — he wasn't going to be much use to him.

"Can I access all the other person's thoughts?"

"The immediate only, sir." Kohler placed his elbows on his desk, steepled his fingers, and rested his lips against the tips of them.

"You may go."

Kohler stayed in that position for a while — he was disappointed he couldn't access Cassia's memories. He would have enjoyed replaying her fear from when they were in his office in Camburg, finding out her darkest secrets to use against her; but no, he could still use this. He'd enjoy tormenting her and he'd enjoy watching her slip up, feeding him her secrets. There was only so much the recruit they called Rage could find out. Part of the problem with the GDO's vision for child soldiers was that they couldn't gain access to briefings, to missions. The ordinary person only sees them as children, and that was an oversight on the GDO's part.

RAGE

Rage fuses two wires together. "Now, this bomb will blow open a door without too much of a kick back for you to worry about getting seriously injured."

Jono and Drummer drink in her tutorial; she can tell they're determined to become bomb experts themselves.

"How come Dune never taught us this stuff?" Jono grumbles.

"Kind of busy running the base here?" Yve suggests.

"Yeah, but this is a useful skill."

"Bombs can be unpredictable," Luca explains. "And some of us aren't career soldiers... well, none of *us* are."

"Speak for yourself," Drummer says primly.

"You joined the army out of boredom and wanting a proper meal instead of crappy rations." Jono rolls his eyes at Drummer.

"So did you." That shuts Jono up and they get back to watching Rage's demonstration. She hopes they are all secretly glad that she turned out to be a spy, because the real Rage is an asset to the team — how much she knows, how much more of a soldier she is than them.

"What's Cass up to?" Shreya asks.

"She's been asked to go on patrol, keeps her away from any decision making. Dune is aware of her predicament and agrees she should be kept out of ops," Luca responds.

"When's our fake meeting?" Drummer looks to Luca for the answer.

"Dorm, tonight, and no mention at all of anything we're thinking of doing. Cass is under enough pressure as it is."

"Has... has he said anything more to her?" Shreya hesitantly asks Luca about Cassia.

"Yes, but she's strong, the initial shock threw her but she's rallied amazingly."

"I can't imagine..." Shreya falls quiet.

"I don't think any of us can, she's probably the only one of us who could endure that." Yve looks pained.

Rage listens to them talk of Cassia, of her bravery, but she knows, as she imagines Luca knows, that it's taking a toll already. It's only been a couple of days but there are dark smudges under Cassia's eyes and she's jumpier than she was before. Rage has also noticed she's pulling away from any intimacy with Luca — if he hugs her, she steps away quickly. She doesn't understand why Cassia is doing this, but then, she is only twelve or thirteen.

Rage makes her way to the farmhouse to help Carl out with prepping food for the evening meal. She walks past the briefing room; the door is open slightly and as she passes, she sees Echo lean in and kiss Dune. Rage rushes by, embarrassed. Even though Echo has been nice to Rage, there's something about her that feels horribly familiar, reminds her of her home, if that's what you call the army base you were brought up on. Maybe it's because she, too, spent a lot of time on a GDO base, working undercover for the Resistance.

Carl hands Rage a basket of carrots to peel and she sets to work. Whilst she peels she talks to Knight, and when he tells her about his encounter with Kohler she nearly peels her finger. She bolts out of the kitchen and out towards the front sentry poit.

Cassia turns when she hears Rage's running feet. "What is it?"

"Kohler asked Knight about the tech."

"It's okay, Rage, he's just gathering information."

"No, you don't understand! He knows who Knight is! He knows who he is! What if he finds out about him helping us? What if he finds out about what I've been doing... he'll then... he'll then..."

Rage begins to shake and the buzzing, buzzing, BUZZING starts up in her head, and then the screams surface.

The third and final time she ran away, she was eleven. They'd tightened security, increased her training, reduced her down time so that she was too exhausted to attempt another escape. She was watched; they knew she was a risk to them, but they still couldn't control her, not like the others. Everyone else was so compliant.

She made it further the third time, all the way to the banks of the river. When they caught her she was ready for whatever torture they threw at her, because she knew that the next time she'd either make it or die; there was no other choice any more. That's when they implanted the Symbio tech into the base of her skull – she was the first test subject. The pain at first was unbearable; the headaches were so severe that she vomited. It seemed like a good attempt at torture, but she'd still run again. And then, when she'd adjusted to the tech and her vision didn't blur as much, and the room didn't swim, they linked her to Knight. They then put her in a room next to him that was soundproofed.

And then they tortured him.

And she could hear it in her head.

His screams were inside her head.

Inside her head. Inside her head. His screams. Inside her head. Inside her head. Inside her head. Knight's screams. Inside her head. Knight's pain. Inside her head. Inside her head. Inside her head. Inside her head. Inside her head. Inside her head. Inside her head. Inside her head. Inside her head. Inside her head. Inside her head. Inside her head. His screams, his screams, his screams. Inside her head. Inside her head. Inside her head. Inside her head. Inside her head.

She did this.

She didn't try to run away again.

CASSIA

Rage is on her knees before me hyperventilating and I don't know what to do. I'm so tired I can't think straight; every dream, every nightmare, every sound wakes me now. I feel like I'm on autopilot as I place my rifle on the ground and kneel before her. Somehow, despite my feeling of detachment, I'm able to understand what's happened.

"They're not going to hurt him, Night is safe."

"They will," she whispers, and she sounds like the frightened child she'd feigned to be when we found her that first day at the petrol station.

"They've hurt him before?" I feel like I'm miles away from my own body but I'm trying to get back because I can see Rage needs me.

"Yes." She looks up at me with those eyes that are the deepest blue, eyes that aren't truly hers, that can be either fire or ice, and for the first time I see the true pain in them. "Inside my head," she says.

My current hell may be one thing, but what they've done to Rage, to this *child,* is beyond what anyone should have to endure. "I'm sorry, Rage, I'm so sorry. What can I do?"

"We have to save him."

I squeeze my eyes shut and I want to scream until I'm hoarse. "Rage…"

"I shouldn't have told you," she realises with horror.

"It's my fault. I should have sent you away, sent you to Yve or Luca." I put my head in my hands. I can't even offer her comfort without putting her in danger. "I won't let Kohler know about him, I promise. I will never let that happen."

She's distraught now. "But your subconscious! You don't understand he's so—"

"Stop! Don't give me details." And it hurts to say it because I can see she wants to tell me, to open up to me, and I have to push her away. "Rae, go to Luca, go tell Luca." She pulls away from me and I can see how lost she feels. "Promise me. You have to tell Luca, the team needs to know, I can't be the one to tell him, I can't think about it anymore."

"Okay." Her voice is small, disappointed; I know that she understands but it doesn't change how hurtful this is.

She walks back towards the mess and I pick up my rifle and turn to survey the landscape before me, so open, so untouched by this war. I try to feel some comfort in it, but all I can feel are the bars of my prison. But I will myself to focus on it, to think about it so that Rage's words slip away as I focus on the details in front of my eyes.

RAGE

Luca is in the mess, and when he sees Rage walk in he gets up immediately and leads her outside to the grove of trees where they'd sat together before.

"What's wrong?" he asks gently.

"I went to Cassia and I shouldn't have, I wasn't thinking." She's distraught; she could have doomed Knight. She tells Luca what she told Cassia and looks at him expectantly.

"We'll factor him and all the others into our plans and Cassia will help when she's able."

Rage slumps against a tree. "What if he's hurt, or worse, because of me?"

"We just have to do everything we can to make sure that doesn't happen."

"What's the plan then?"

"We start by getting Cassia to the doctor Clive found."

"I think you were right not to plan anything against the GDO, I think that's what they'd be expecting."

"Exactly, they think about their victories, we think about our people. Like you, Rae, you're our people."

Rage can't help but smile at that. "Thanks."

"And when Cassia is back to being Cassia, we're going to start putting together a plan to free Night."

"She's not doing too good."

Luca's brave façade cracks at that. "No, she's not."

They sit in silence for a while, enjoying the comfort of just having someone near.

Sault team are sitting at the end of their beds, looking oddly uniform and soldierly for once. Rage can't help looking at Cassia, worried for her because she looks like she's about to crack.

Cassia's voice is weak when she speaks, her exhaustion now hard to hide. "The only way I can see to fix it is to kill Kohler. With him dead, I can live with the implant in me without any problems. But, we need to remove and destroy his so that no one else can access my link. Knowing Kohler, he hasn't broadcast what he's done."

"Do we know where he is?" Jono asks. Rage doesn't say anything, playing the part of the spy. This theatre is what Cassia will be pretending to forget; nothing can give them away.

"We can track down their headquarters easily enough." Yve shrugs, as though it's no big deal.

"Yve, you get on that. We need to act fast. I don't know how long I can keep this up." There's far too much truth to Cassia's words.

After a few more instructions, they all begin to get ready to turn in. Cassia lies on top of her bed in her gear and closes her eyes. Rage slides under her sheets and watches her, wonders how much sleep she'll get. She remembers how after what they did to Knight she didn't sleep properly for months and months, and even now she is haunted in her dreams by his screams. She falls asleep, praying that her demons are quiet tonight, because to save Knight, they have to save Cassia first.

CASSIA

I get two hours of sleep before he wakes me. My eyes feel like they're filled with gluey sand and I'm desperately thirsty. I sit up and drink from my canteen as he speaks. Now is my chance.

"Aren't you sleeping, Cassia?"

"I was, until you came along." The back of my mind whispers, *"Don't think about the plan, don't think about the plan."*

I can feel his smirk, but I ignore how it makes my insides turn to liquid. *"Don't you enjoy our reunion, Fortis? We always had something, don't you think?"*

"We never had a thing, just me beating you, over and over again." I make it sound like I'm feeling smug, but in reality I'm gripping my water bottle far too tightly and focusing incredibly hard. I keep my eyes on the rim of the flask, because if I look up and someone is awake, I don't know if I'll be able to do this with their acknowledgement of my struggle. My mind continues to whisper, *"Don't think about the plan, about ripping his chip out, don't think about it."*

"I don't believe you've ever beaten me, only given me more cause to pursue you. Oh, the things I want to do to you." He sends me visuals then, something I didn't know the link could do. My hands begin to shake. I have to stay focused, even throughout his vile imaginings

of me and him, of what he would do to my body. It feels impossible and then, inexplicably, I hear his own subconscious and I grab hold of it, blocking out the visuals as hard I can and I listen, listen, listen.

"I'm assuming you like to be that rough because of what your daddy did to you?" The visuals stop abruptly.

"What did you say?"

"How did your subconscious put it? Oh yes, 'I'll be in control now, I'll show him that I can be the master.' How often did he beat you? Daily?"

"You know nothing about me, Fortis."

"Oh yes I do. You forget I'm inside your head too, Kohler. I know you, I know all about you." He drops the link instantly, and I take in a shuddering breath and then look up to see Luca watching me from his bed.

"It's done," I say to him. He nods but not to me, to someone behind me. Before I can react, I feel a sharp scratch on my shoulder. I look up at Yve as she lowers me to the bed.

"It's all going to be okay, Cass, we've got you."

"Thank you," I manage to slur as I go under.

RAGE

They move quickly once Cassia is out. The team dresses, and Luca carries Cassia out to the truck that Ham has ready and waiting. They included him and Dune in their plan but that was all, not wanting to involve the entire base. Rage is surprised to find Dune in the back, helping Luca secure Cassia.

"You're coming with us?"

"Sault team is my team, too." He smiles at Rage and she grins back, feeling relieved that they're taking action once again. The entire team is loaded into the truck and they head towards Naevena, whose border is close to their location in Old France. Naevena has regained some control — although Degeland is still under GDO control. It's the safest and closest location they could risk taking Cassia.

It takes three hours for them to arrive in Bernhem. The hospital is under Resistance guard — Jono, Drummer, Ham, and Shreya join the patrol on security. Yve takes the hospital reception, Dune covers the lifts, and Luca and Rage are allowed to wait outside the operating theatre.

"Why do you think they're giving her such good treatment? They don't know her."

"Well, partly because of what she did for the Resistance and partly because inside her head is a direct link to a GDO major and the only working Symbio implant we have. They may be able to link up to Kohler or even hack the tech and find out their secrets."

"So it's not that they care about human life?" Rage states, sardonically.

"They do, but this is a big risk for the hospital in a safe zone. They need to have good reason to put the rest of the patients in danger."

"Do you think that one day people will just want to help other people out of kindness, not out of a need to... to... self-service? Does that make sense?" She turns to Luca with a confused, childlike look on her face.

"Makes total sense and yes, I think people will be kind again for the sake of being kind."

"Imagine a world like that."

"It sort of was a world like that, until..."

"It all went to shit."

"Language."

Rage scowls at him. "I'm a soldier, I don't need to mind my language."

"You're twelve, yes you do."

"Or thirteen."

"You're too small to be thirteen." The corner of Luca's mouth cracks into a smile.

"No I'm not, I'm just short, it's a heritage thing, my mum was Japanese." She shrugs.

"And your dad?"

"Not sure but he was tall and blonde, I remember that much... Shame I didn't inherit his height." She frowns.

"You grew up in France, right? Did the GDO teach you English then?" Rage nods and then sighs.

"How long is this going to take?" She puts her elbow on the armrest of her chair and props her cheek against her fist.

"Hours."

"Hours?! But they just have to slice it open real quick like Ian did and then pull it out."

"I think it's the disconnecting safely that'll take time."

Rage huffs with disappointment.

They'd been waiting an hour when they hear running footsteps with a heavy wheeze carried along with it. Luca looks up, alert, and Rage glances up to see a large, pale man shuffling, not really running after all, towards them.

"Clive?" Luca says, bemused.

"How is she?" he replies.

"What are you doing here?"

"I couldn't just sit at home, not knowing what was happening."

Luca's appears too shocked to speak and so Rage sticks out her hand. "I'm Rae."

Clive takes her hand in his soft clammy one. "Clive. Good to finally meet you."

"How did you get here?" Luca asks.

"Mum drove me. She's just flirting with that Dune guy downstairs. So embarrassing." Clive squeezes into a chair and wipes his brow. "Any news?"

"Nothing yet."

"I was also hoping I'd get a look at the tech — they have quite a big Resistance intelligence hub here in Bernhem."

"See, what did I tell you? No one is ever kind for kindness' sake anymore," Rage grumbles.

"What do you mean? I'd do anything for Cass," Clive states.

"I know you would, mate, Rae is just tetchy because she's bored."

"And hungry," Rage complains.

"I brought supplies." Clive pulls some chocolate bars from what can best be described as his fishing vest.

"Chocolate?!" Rage exclaims with delight.

"I have boxes stashed." Rage's opinion of Clive instantly changes. "Here, take your pick." Rage selects a bar and Luca takes one, too.

"Do you think Cass can have one when she wakes up?" Rage asks Clive.

"Now that, Rae, is kindness if ever I saw it." She grins at Luca, chocolate-coated teeth bared.

It's three more hours before the surgeon emerges from the operating room. Rage sits bolt upright in her chair, rigid with anticipation.

"We managed to remove the device and the patient seems to be doing well. We need to check her cognitive ability once she comes around, keep her in for a couple of nights, but it went as well as we hoped."

"Thank you, doctor," Luca says, relieved.

"And the device?" Clive asks.

"We'll clean it up and hand it over. We have contacted a member of our network to come and collect it." The doctor goes back through a set of double doors and Luca relaxes, but only a little.

"When can we see her?" Rage asks.

"They'll bring her past us and put her in a recovery ward," Luca tells her.

"How do you know that?"

"I asked a nurse when you were napping."

"I didn't nap!" Rage crosses her arms.

"Rae, you snored like a bulldog."

"Did not!"

A man walks down the corridor. He has greyish hair and is wearing glasses and a rumpled shirt.

"I'm here for a collection," he remarks to the trio staring at him.

Clive stands up. "I'm AcidFire69. I'd like to help you work on the device."

"RaiderKing69." The man grins and shakes Clive's hand.

"What is happening?" Rage whispers to Luca.

Luca's brow is furrowed. "Dark web code names I'm guessing."

"Ohhhh." She sits back and watches as the two men get acquainted face-to-face, complimenting each other on bits of code, online hacks, and other boring things that Rage doesn't really care about.

A doctor in scrubs comes through the double doors with a small white plastic item with wires sticking out of it in a sealed bag. He hands it over to the intelligence operative who then leaves with Clive in tow, promising he'll be back when Cassia's awake.

"It's gross to think that was in Cass's brain."

Rage pulls a face. "Scary gross." Rage nods in agreement with Luca. It definitely is scary gross.

Luca lowers his voice. "You still get 'coms through, missions and stuff?"

"All the time." Rage gives Luca a serious look. "Why?"

"What are you telling them, what are they telling you?"

"Well, they want me to get in on any new missions, which means Kohler wants me to join the team that's going to go and 'kill' him. I said I was working on finding a way for them to want a child to work with them. I told them I was going to offer myself as a diversion to their plan."

"Smart."

"Don't sound surprised." Rage crossed her arms and frowned at him. "Just because I'm young doesn't mean I'm not capable, if not more so, than the lot of you."

"Oh, I know it. I would never think that, Rae."

"Good."

Fifteen minutes later, two nurses wheel Cassia past them on a bed. She is still unconscious and drooling a little bit. The nurses allow them to sit with her, clearly not wanting to refuse the Resistance fighters, even if one of them is a child. Rage starts getting fidgety again, so Luca tells her to give Dune an update. Cassia begins to stir just as Rage leaves the room, so she darts back in instantly.

"Hey, you." Luca leans forward so that Cassia can see him without having to move.

Cassia snuffles a little bit.

"They got it out, Cass!" Rage says excitedly. Cassia manages a lopsided grin.

"How do you feel?" Luca asks.

Cassia licks her lips and speaks thickly, slurring, "Like my head's been split open."

"Go back to sleep, rest. We'll be here." Luca kisses her forehead as Cassia closes her eyes again.

"She looks pretty when she's sleeping," Rage observes, and then becomes mortified for saying such a thing.

"Go tell, Dune, will you?"

"Sure." Rage leaves the room but looks back and catches Luca crying into Cassia's hand. She decides to stay away for a little while.

WEEK TWENTY-EIGHT

CASSIA

When I wake up Luca is sitting next to me.

"What's going on?" I feel a bit sick and my head hurts, but nothing too severe.

"You had surgery."

"Surgery?"

"We drugged you with a sedative the doctor recommended, drove you here, had you operated on, and voila, you're implant free."

"Really?" I smile at him, a weight lifting from me at his words.

"Really, really." He smiles back as he grips my hand.

Rage races into the room. "You're awake!"

"She's hardly slept all night," Luca tells Rage gently.

"I've been here all night?" I'm surprised; I feel like I fell asleep five minutes ago. I'm not sure why Luca thinks I slept badly; I don't remember waking up once.

"I got you breakfast." Rage hands me a chocolate bar, a huge grin on her face.

"No way, a chocolate bar!"

"I know!" She beams at me and I don't have the heart to tell her I don't feel like eating right now.

"Are the others back at the farmhouse?"

"No, they're all here, waiting for you to wake up. We're going to stay a few days, see what they can find out from the implant."

"Everyone came?" I feel overwhelmed by the thought that they would do that for me.

"Dune and Ham too," Rage adds. I try really hard not to cry.

"See, Rae, that was kindness for kindness' sake," Luca says.

"Oh yeah, I suppose it was." She smiles. "I'm going to let them all know you're awake." She runs out the door.

"She seems like a normal kid all of a sudden," I observe.

"I think it's the sugar high, Clive has been feeding her chocolate bars since he got here."

"Clive's here, too?"

"Wanted to check in on you, and he's been helping out with the Resistance intelligence division here." For some reason the fact that even Clive made it here is the triggering factor and I begin to cry big ugly sobs of relief and gratitude.

"I have no idea why I'm crying," I laugh through my tears, and Luca climbs onto my bed and laughs with me, and I can hear his own relief in the sound of his happiness.

Throughout the day, members of Sault come in to see me and as the day goes on, I feel stronger and stronger. Without my mind being tormented and my body not having to adapt to a device in my skull, I almost feel like myself. I know that what Kohler did to me is going to have some repercussions, but at this point, I allow myself to feel relief, to think freely without the fear of him listening in.

Yve is one of the last to come to visit me. "For a minute there, I thought you'd die." I turn my head carefully and see Yve looking down at me with both a pissed off and completely freaked out look on her face.

"I might have, just a little."

"Such a show off." She's frowning, and of course, it's prettily, because it's Yve.

"What's the news on the device?"

"Clive and the team down there haven't slept, they said they'd come and debrief us in here, seeing as you have a private room and he insisted you were at the briefing." I'm grateful to him for that; after all, the thing was inside my head.

Two hours later, I'm feeling even better. I'd insisted on washing and the nurse refused me a shower but Luca offered to give me a bed bath instead. She'd glared at him disapprovingly until I informed her he was my boyfriend and I was comfortable with it. I felt pathetic and wholly exposed as he carefully cleaned my body. But he was gentle and tender and I knew that he needed to feel like he was helping me in some way. And he was; he was washing away the feeling of Kohler crawling inside my skin.

It's odd being in bed whilst everyone else is standing around in uniform — I am very conscious of my flimsy, arse-less gown, despite being under covers. Clive and a man in glasses, who I don't know, share a look. The man in glasses nods and Clive starts to speak.

"We've been able to trace where the signal is received." This would have been exciting news but we already know where the base is — Rage had told us when she confessed her involvement with the GDO. However, this does mean we don't have to find a way of telling the Resistance what we already know, keeping Rage's secret safe for a little longer.

"Does the device still work? Can we programme it to feed false information to him?" I ask.

"Actually, that's what I want to ask you." Clive looks uncomfortable.

"It's okay, go on."

"We can refit it as an external attachment, behind your ear, like a wireless ear piece." I must not be able to hide how that makes me feel because he rushes on, "You won't have to wear it all the time. You can take it off and we'll rig it to alert you when you're receiving a message by linking it up to your tablet."

"Will it work the same?"

"It'll be more like their 'com device for him — he won't be able to tap into any of your thoughts, he'll only hear what you want him to hear."

"Can you turn it around quickly enough?" Dune asks. "Surely this down time will be suspicious to him?"

"I could feed hints that I was knocked out because you tried to remove it, but couldn't. Can I still layer messages?"

"I don't know, I suppose that's up to your own skill with the device."

"If you can, Cassia, it would be an enormous help." Dune's expression is kind, knowing that what they're asking is hard for me.

"I'll do whatever I can." Because, let's be honest, I'll face that man any way I can if it means I'm closer to destroying him.

"Anything else that can help us?" Dune asks.

The man with glasses responds. "This tech is very advanced, we can use it to implement cyber illusions – make them believe we have more personnel, launch false attacks, create viruses even Clive hasn't dreamt up yet."

"Do what you can but get that implant back to Cassia quickly. I don't want the other side getting suspicious," Dune instructs, and they both leave to do as he says, and just like that the meeting is over.

They all leave until it's just me, Dune, Luca, and Rage, who we can't seem to get rid of now.

"So, now we just wait?" Luca says to Dune.

"We wait, but I want to be absolutely sure you're okay with this, Cassia." Dune says to me.

"I want him beaten and gone — I will do whatever it takes," I reply.

"I appreciate that, we all appreciate that, but you may not realise the toll it's taking on you." I don't think I'd ever thought Dune would be so considerate, as I've always seen him as our leader first, putting the Resistance's agenda above everything.

Luca takes my hand. "No one wants you to put yourself through too much, Cass."

"I'll be in worse shape if I don't do anything, so I'm doing this. Got it?"

"Okay, got it." Luca squeezes my hand.

Dune turns to leave but Rage is giving him a funny look. "Yes, Rae?"

"What's your real name?" she asks.

"My real name? Why?"

"Wondering." She shrugs at him.

"Nic."

"Your real name is Nick?"

"Yes." He frowns at her but it doesn't deter her line of questioning.

"Oh, that's just... so disappointing. Dune just made you sound kind of cool and mysterious, now you're just... ordinary."

"Right, okay. See you later, guys." Dune leaves us to go back on duty.

"I get why he chooses to call himself Dune, now. Like, I bet my real name is super lame too. Like, Kate or Jin."

"Wait, you don't remember your real name?" I look at Rage bewildered as she shakes her head matter-of-factly. "But you remember your mum."

"Don't remember her name either. Don't know why, just don't."

"It must be because of what happened," I say gently, but Rage just shrugs.

"I'm going to see Jono and Drummer, see what I can trade for some chocolate."

"I hope you asked Clive for that stash in your pocket," I yell after her when I see the bulge of contraband.

"Yeah, yeah," she mutters as she leaves.

"Should we, like, give her rules, like you would a normal kid?" Luca looks after her with a confused, almost bewildered expression on his face.

"I think she's a force unto herself. We have no hope of doing anything to discipline that one. I think what she needs most is our friendship."

Luca climbs onto the bed and lies down next to me.

"What's with us always being in tiny beds?" I observe.

"The curse of an army relationship, I guess." He rests his head against mine. "How are you really doing?"

"Honestly, I don't know. I'm happy it's out, but... the things he said, the *images* he sent."

Luca flinches. "Images?"

"I just hope I can forget. I really, really hope I can forget."

"If you can't, you learn to keep going forward, okay?"

"So long as I've got you."

"Urgh." I turn to look at the door to where Rage is standing.

"Thought you were pestering Jono and Drummer?" I can't hide the slight irritation from my tone, annoyed that she overheard our private conversation.

"They're sleeping… Can I teach you how to make a bomb? I brought supplies." She brings out hospital supplies from behind her back.

"Uh, Luc, you can take this one."

RAGE

Rage is relieved when they leave the hospital the following day — it was getting pretty boring there, despite the chocolate. They are heading back to the farmhouse, deciding it is better to stay there knowing the GDO are watching than to move out to a new, pre-arranged location when the time is right. This way they can control the situation as much as they can. Dune told them that they had to focus on their original plan and start implementing it — the Resistance unit had successfully interrupted supply chains, begun rallying civilians, and disabled some defences, but it was time to increase their offensive. When they returned to the farmhouse, they were going to work as one unit and take out supplies, disable three GDO bases, and then start moving towards Troyes, rallying support as they go. Other Resistance units across the country were doing the same, targeting larger towns within the region, building momentum towards the final push, Old Paris. And once Old Paris was retaken, they will have control of Old France once more and finally they can begin their offensive and make their way towards Utonia, the GDO's main country of operation, the core of the regime.

"This is it, we're about to push towards our goal. I need you all fit and focused."

"Yes, sir," they say in unison, and the energy in the back of the truck changes, but Cassia doesn't appear to have been able to muster the same enthusiasm. Rage watches her as she grips the small, silicone-coated device and her tablet. The tablet pings — a new message. Everyone falls silent. Cassia slips the refashioned implant over her right ear and closes her eyes to concentrate. Rage looks over Cassia's shoulder and reads the automatic transcript that's now being logged so it can be analysed for any missed information or hidden clues. As Rage reads, she hopes for Cassia's sake that whoever reads the conversation is sympathetic to Cassia's situation. Rage looks away ashamed for seeing what has been tormenting Cassia, and she knows it's only a small part of what she has endured. To Cassia's right, Luca holds her hand and reads the messages with a calm that Rage knows he must be working really hard to show. Because right now, all Rage wants to do is blow something up. That Kohler guy, whoever he is, is a pig, and Rage can think of a lot of things she'd like to do to repay him for the things he imagines doing to Cassia.

Rage is plotting her revenge, which involves a strategically placed, small explosive device, when they finally reach the farmhouse. Echo is there to greet them and looks relieved to see everyone back, but Rage catches the look she gives Dune. Clearly he'd neglected to tell her where they were going and Rage wonders about that — maybe things aren't so good between the two of them, or maybe Dune puts his team's needs before his girlfriends. Cassia has become increasingly paranoid and has begged everyone not to let anyone else in on what happened, to make them think she's still wired up. Rage thinks Cassia is being overly cautious, and maybe acting a little unhinged. Everyone has agreed to keep Cassia's secret, even though they don't think there could be a mole in the camp, seeing as most of them are aware that the mole has already been uncovered. But then again, muses Rage as she makes her way to the kitchen to see what food she can steal, she wouldn't put it past the GDO having five spies in the same camp at once. They do like overkill.

She makes her way up the stairs, and passing Dune's room she pauses and listens.

"What's going on? You never keep me out of the loop. Since when were you secretive?" Echo's voice is clipped and bitter.

"I'm not being secretive, we tried to help Cassia and couldn't." Dune sounds placating.

"You left without telling me what you were doing, what is it about this team of teenagers that has you running all over the place?"

"Leila…" *Leila?* Rage mouthed. "Come on, I saw an opportunity to visit the intelligence base there. Don't be pissed off because you're feeling left out… I'll make it up to you."

Rage clamps her hands over her mouth and accidentally sends Knight a message as she creeps away and up towards her old room.

"What's ick?"

"Two soldiers about to be… intimate."

"Ick. How did it all go?"

"She's doing okay but we need to find a way to destroy this guy who's our new Major. He's… well… he's not someone we want to keep around."

"What can I do?"

"Find out whatever you can, but discreetly."

"No problem!" Rage doesn't like how excited Knight sounds at the prospect of putting his neck on the line.

"I changed my mind, can't you get a hobby or something?"

"A hobby? In this place? Like what?"

"I don't know, counting ceiling tiles." Rage uses her sleeve to wipe the dust off the frame of an old mirror in the attic.

"I'm going to be fine."

"I think I should come back, I'd be happier if I was there with you. I'll find a way to get pulled out."

"But if you're here then there won't be any exciting stories for you to tell me and for me to be jealous of. Hey, promise something?"

"What?" Rage is always suspicious of promises Knight wants, and they usually end up being something she thoroughly disagrees with.

"You'll teach me that hippo game when you get back... but after you've blown up the base. You are planning on blowing it up, right?"

"Oh totally, it's just... I'm sorry, Knight, it can't be yet. They think that's what Kohler will expect."

Knight tries to make it sound like he isn't bothered, but in his head he can't hide his true feelings from her. *"It's no big deal, wouldn't want to miss out on Mysterious Stew Tuesday anyway."*

"Who would, all that fat and gristle... yuuuuuum."

"You'll... you'll come back soon though, right?"

His hesitancy makes her heart ache. *"I'll be first through the door the second we come up with a plan that won't harm you or any of the other snot rags."*

"You're so mean about them, they aren't that bad."

"Jared NAMED himself Jared. They're pretty bad."

"He's annoying, but not everyone is terrible. Like, oh, what's her name..."

"Elliot? Yeah, she's nice."

"Ellie, that's it." Rage feels a squeeze of jealousy but not *that* kind; she just wants to keep Knight to herself. At least he can't speak with Elliot the way she can speak to him.

"She messages me all the time."

Oh well, Rage thought, she's eager, this Ellie. Puny arms though, if Rage recalls correctly — couldn't load a rifle that quickly either. And yes, couldn't wire a bomb for love nor money, and nearly lost her finger. It is a shame she hadn't, then she couldn't work in the basement with Knight.

"That's nice…" Rage looks out the window and sees Jono and Drummer heading to the mess by doing forward rolls. She runs down all the stairs, barely paying attention to Knight as he describes his interactions with doe-eyed Elliot. She races ahead of them and they pause, post roll, seated.

"Whatchya doing?"

"Seeing how many roly-polys it takes to get from the farmhouse to the mess, obviously," Jono explains.

Rage calculates the distance. "For you or me?"

"Both." Drummer squints at her in assessment.

"Twenty-five for you, twenty-eight for me," she estimates, and then starts at the farmhouse until she has caught up with them.

"What you doing, Rae, you've gone all quiet but grunty?"

"Forward roll competition. Need to concentrate."

"I wish you'd brought me with you," Knight sighs, and then has to listen as Rage counts her rolls.

When Rage reaches the mess, relatively dizzy and landing with her legs halfway up the wall, she looks up to see Luca staring down at her. "Twenty-nine," he says.

"What did the boys do?"

"Squirt, you can't call us boys," Drummer scolds.

"How many?"

"Twenty-three," Luca replies.

"Who won?" Rage asks, and Jono and Drummer give each other a look that says they will never live this one down.

"You did," Jono sighs.

Rage jumps up in victory and then stumbles to the side, still dizzy.

"I've just eaten a brie baguette, it messed up my rolling. I would have definitely done tighter ones otherwise," Drummer complains to Jono.

"Look, we just have to face it, we got beaten by a sort of thirteen-year-old who makes bombs."

"All I ever did when I was thirteen or so was w—"

Jono interrupts Drummer quickly, "We're all too aware what you got up to, but let's not scar the kid, yeah?" Laughing, they head into the mess for their last evening off before they begin their mission in earnest. It is time for them to take real action against their enemy. It is time to fight back.

WEEK TWENTY-NINE

CASSIA

Sitting in the mess, I'm trying to distract myself from thinking about Kohler, about what he wants with me, and so I'm listening to the others joking around, finding time to relax before we plunge ourselves back into this war. The farmhouse has been too much of a bubble, despite what I've experienced. We feel sheltered here, at home. It's a dangerous feeling when you're fighting for freedom; it makes you complacent. It's time to work with the rest of the base and the rest of the Resistance. It's not just Sault in one corner interacting tonight; it's most of the people here. We've kept ourselves too apart, and now is the time for us to feel like a piece of the bigger picture.

I use my recovery as an excuse to duck out early as I contemplate what re-entering this war really means to me. I do want to fight the GDO, now possibly more than ever, but I doubt myself. I fear my own cowardice and inability to do whatever it takes. I don't know if I have that in me, especially now, after I've been shaken to my core. Luca catches up to me.

"Going to bed without me? Incredibly rude, Cassia."

"Actually, I had an idea."

"Yeah?" He raises his eyebrows at me.

"I was thinking of pushing our beds together. I could... I could do with you close right now."

He kisses my temple. "Of course." And instantly his flirtation evaporates and he's the kind and supportive man I've come to rely upon.

The next morning we receive post from Vayo along with a handful of new recruits. A letter from my parents is handed over; Luca has one from his, as well. As we're reading, there's a cough from behind us. I turn, and I don't know how to react when I see who has decided to join us. Luca turns, too, and lets out what I can only describe as a bellow and runs to his brother. Ellyas is standing before us, looking more like his old self, more assured. Since he'd decided to join Jake in his fight against the Resistance, he'd lost his way a little, but now, he's finally come back to Luca.

"It's good to see you." Luca gives him a hug.

"I've brought you something." He carefully pulls out a brown package from his backpack and unwraps some of Luca's mum's oat biscuits. "I didn't even eat one." Luca hugs him again, possibly a little more enthusiastically than before.

"You sure about this?" Luca says through a mouthful of cookie.

"I'm better now and things are pretty settled in Vayo. I wanted something to do." He gives Luca's shoulder a reassuring squeeze.

I go over and give him a hug. "We have a lot to fill you in on," I say, and give Luca a meaningful look. I don't want to be the one to do it.

"I'll show you around." Luca leads Ellyas away and I feel a lightness I hadn't expected, Luca having someone there for him instead of him having to spend all his time and energy worrying about me. I hadn't realised until then how much I take him for granted, how much he needed his brother here.

The new members are briefed and we are all sent to prep for our mission. We're shaking things up today and going out during daylight — by changing our mode of operation we'll be, hopefully, taking the GDO by surprise. Sault team is to disable one of three bases, which we're all attacking simultaneously. We all gather on the grass as Dune instructs us on which units will be working together. "Sault, you're with me and Unit 5; Ellyas, you'll be joining Sault team seeing as you know a lot of them already."

Unit 5 comprises of the more experienced soldiers, the ones who were in the army before this war and was commanded by Dune; Ham, Ian, and Echo are also part of the team. As the newest and youngest team, it's no surprise we've been put with Unit 5. But by pairing up with Dune, I know instantly that we're taking the largest base, the one that's closest to Troyes. I put the refashioned Symbio device on my ear so I can respond to any messages without having to take my tablet. Having Kohler in my head might be an added problem to my already shaky trigger finger, but I'm hoping it will focus my anger into something more useful.

Only one group is on foot — the rest of us clamber into the back of the vehicles that once belonged to the GDO, and we start our convoy. We're divided into three trucks for our mission, the biggest I've been on yet, which makes me more anxious. Rage is in uniform, expertly shortened by Jono — Dune didn't want to bring her along, but Sault refused to leave her behind. He told us she had to stay in the truck; little does he know that the explosives we've provided for the mission were built by Rage, with some help from Jono and Drummer. I have one tucked into the front pocket of my jacket, and honestly, being jostled about with a bomb next to your boob is a little nerve-racking, especially if it could be one that Jono or Drummer helped make.

The drive is long. We stop an hour out to relieve ourselves and eat some rations in preparation. Rage is pestering Ian to teach her some of his knife skills, and he's doing his best to ignore her constant chatter, but I can tell he's getting really frustrated with her. I call her over and notice her pockets are bulging.

"Bombs or chocolate?"

She pats her pockets. "Bit of both."

"And you're absolutely sure that this will only blow a door?" I point to my breast bomb.

"Of course I am." She frowns at me. "Don't you trust me?"

"I trust you completely — I'm just not that keen on explosives."

"Oh, you don't need to worry about a Betsy bomb, they are very localised and stable."

I feel a little reassured and try not to think that I'm trusting a child with bomb expertise. "Betsy?"

"Seems like a Betsy, gets the job done with minimum fuss."

"Any named after yourself?"

Her smile is wide and vicious. "Haven't made one big enough to justify it yet." And for that, I'm relieved.

The second leg of our journey feels like it takes no time at all. We jump out the back of the truck one by one and nobody speaks. We know our commands, but we have our radios if we need confirmation or if Dune has any orders. We divide up, as planned. Rage sits in the back of the truck, grudgingly. I wonder how long she'll stay there.

Dune, Echo, Luca, Ellyas, Yve, and I head for the front entrance to what was a French barracks and is now used as a GDO army barracks. This is our hardest target yet. The wire fence isn't particularly threatening, but the huge contingent of guards on duty is. This is where our plan comes in. We're dressed in GDO uniform, and Yve is wearing Shreya's old one. I've put the Symbio implant in my pocket and my hair is in a ponytail, exposing my scar. We climb into a smaller vehicle and drive towards the front entrance. Dune and I are in the front, the others in the back.

The soldiers on duty stop us and ask for ID.

"We had to steal this truck, we ran into some trouble with the Resistance, all our documentation was in the other one." Dune tells the guards.

"I need you both to step out of the vehicle." We do as requested. We didn't expect to get through that easily.

"I need to deliver this soldier to your commanding officer — she's part of an experimental programme." Dune speaks as though he's in charge; it's effective.

"What's the programme called? I'll speak to my commander."

"You don't have clearance for that," Dune barks.

I mutter, "Symbio." The soldier hears and Dune whips around to face me.

"Why they ever decided to test this out on such a green recruit is beyond me. When I say they don't have clearance I mean keep your goddamn mouth shut, woman!"

I clamp my mouth shut and we wait as they radio in. "Boss says he's very interested in this Simbo thingy. He'll meet you in the compound."

We climb back into the truck and drive through the gates. "This is why the GDO are weak, they just don't train their people properly." Dune's expression is dark as he talks.

"I think you'll find that we are excellent soldiers, considering our training," I respond.

"That's because you had common sense to begin with, some of these recruits are painfully dumb, and without proper training and drilling they're just going to get themselves killed."

"You seem upset."

"I don't take taking lives lightly. It's necessary for the freedom of our nations but it's never easy, especially when the opposition are young and clueless."

I let out a weary sigh. "I know how you feel. A lot of soldiers signed up as it was the safest option."

"Not all of them, though, we have to remember that." Dune's jaw clenches tightly shut.

Dune pulls up outside a sand-coloured brick building and we're escorted to the door by Echo, Ellyas, Luca, and Yve. We're led through the main entrance by a GDO soldier and the major in charge greets us. We've removed our radios, helmets, and packs; otherwise, we look too much like we're going into combat. This is the riskiest move we're making, because of our lack of equipment and our face-to-face with the enemy.

"You're the one with the chip?" the major asks. He's the oldest major I've met, near retirement, if I'm correct.

"Yes, sir." I turn my head so he can glimpse my scar. He extends his arm towards the staircase and begins to walk. We follow.

"Large contingent for one little chip."

"It's our first fully operational model — it needs protecting," Dune replies.

"I thought a pair of children had it."

I cut in before Dune can show his ignorance. "They do, sir, but there was an issue, the link is entirely between the two of them, there's no listening in. This one..." I tap the side of my neck.

"This one is fully traceable, all conversations can be monitored."

"Bit of an oversight putting that tech in two children if they can't listen in, don't you think?"

"It was, but then again, it was new technology, it was impossible to test any other way."

He opens the door to his office and Dune and I step in. Dune instructs the others to wait outside. Echo frowns at the order but complies. He closes the door gently and then, as he turns his back, Dune steps forward and slides his knife straight through the back of the major's neck, where my scar is. I wonder if the choice of execution style was on purpose. Dune holds his hand over the major's mouth as he gurgles out his last, bloody breaths. I don't look at the body as Dune lets it sag to the ground.

I remove my radio 'com from inside my jacket, as does Dune. "Ready to move out?" I nod. We only have our side arms and ES guns, and our rifles are also, sadly, in the truck. But we needed access before the others could move in.

"Time to move." We open the door and the rest of the team are wearing their 'coms and moving up the stairs, heading to the control room. There are too many soldiers in this compound for us to take on, and so we're going to lock as many of them as we can into their barracks whilst we take out the rest of the base. The other Resistance fighters are waiting for our signal to move.

The map Clive sent us is clear in my mind as we make our way along the second floor corridor of the main building, the one where senior officers are based. This means fewer bodies to get in our way and it is also the hub of their operation. Echo strangles a surprised soldier, a fierce, unforgiving look on her face, and we carry on moving forward.

We breach the door of the security room with a small controlled blast from Betsy — the noise is going to bring soldiers from all over the building and compound to us, and so we have to act fast. I take in the room. It's larger than I'd pictured from the blueprints. Yve begins activating security protocols and locks the barracks off. Dune is just about to speak his orders to the other soldiers when I see something out of the corner of my eye; I spin and fire, grazing the neck of the GDO soldier who has happened upon us. No, wait, more are approaching; I don't understand how they've mobilised so fast. Then the 'coms come through — *"Boss, it's an ambush! They knew we were coming."*

"Fall back. FALL BACK," Dune orders, and I feel sick. All our people, the rest of our team, are out there. My attention focuses back on the room and I realise I should be worrying about our situation as well, because ten soldiers have their guns trained on

us. We drop our weapons as instructed and back towards the wall.

I'm breathing heavily, and Luca shifts so he's standing beside me.

"This feels oddly familiar," he whispers.

"At least we have some company this time."

"True, but that company happens to be the same people who saved our arses last time."

"I knew there was something I was missing." I reach out and find his hand.

But there was something I was forgetting — that little glint of light I'd seen as I'd surveyed the compound before we headed inside.

The first explosion rings out and only disturbs a few dust motes within the room. The second blows out the wall where the soldiers are standing. The third is percussive and shakes the foundations of the building. These all happen within split seconds of each other. Rage had been hiding underneath the truck and that's what had caught my eye — the glint of lights from one of the bombs peeking out of her top pocket. I'd never been more relieved to have a bomb-making young girl on our team before.

Most of the soldiers are taken down by the blast; three are able to recover, but Dune and Echo take them out instantly. We move.

We make our way over dead bodies and debris to the half-obliterated hallway. Luca, Ellyas, Dune, and Echo grab rifles. There isn't one for me. We run along the corridor towards the stairs, and when we reach the staircase we notice that below us the second blast seems to have taken out most of the west wing of the building — if Rage still hasn't named a bomb after herself, I am seriously dreading the kind of destruction one named after her could cause, especially as Rae couldn't have hidden something with that much explosive power in her combat trouser pockets. I'll ask her about it later — right now, we need to move and find Rae. I try her on the radio we'd insisted she wear, grumbling about it because she already had enough "voices in her head", but she doesn't answer.

"Cassia, why are you calling Rae?" Dune demands.

"Who do you think makes our bombs?"

To do Dune credit, he doesn't stop running as I drop that piece of information on him.

"When we get back to base we need to have a serious discussion."

"Yes, boss."

The structure of the foyer looks unsound and the front door is blocked off, so we head towards the eastern wing to try to find an exit. We have to navigate round some rubble and that's where we find Rae; she's slumped against the wall, her arm scorched, and her jacket melted to some of her skin.

I kneel down in front of her. "Rae…? RAE!" I can tell she's breathing but she's unresponsive, so I gently feel the back of her head and there's a large lump. She must have been knocked back by the blast.

"Luc, can you carry her?" Without a word, he bends down and picks her up. We make our way along the corridor into a room at the furthest end of the building. Luca sets Rae down on a sofa and we survey the situation outside. GDO troops are gathering.

"We're trapped," Dune says, and I don't allow my fear to rise. We need to get Rae out of here; we need to get her to a doctor.

I look around the room and I can't see a medical kit. I don't know for how long we'll be trapped, and so I head for the door.

"What are you doing?" Dune demands.

"I'm going to see what I can find for her burns whilst you guys figure out how to get us out of this."

"Cassia, you need to start acting like a soldier, ask permission, follow my orders, otherwise you'll jeopardise the rest of the team." I'm chastened by his words but he adds, "Go see what you can find."

Remembering how my mum took care of my leg after I knocked boiling water onto it a few years ago, I make a mental list of what I'm going to need: somewhere to bathe her wounds in warm water, cling film, and scissors. Basically, I need a kitchen. I just hope Rage didn't blow up the wing that had the kitchen in it.

Of course, the door I need is the one that's warped from the blast, but after three kicks, I manage to break it open. It's not the main kitchen but it is a small kitchenette. The sink is small but there's a washing up bucket that I fill with lukewarm water, the scissors are in with the cutlery, and by some miracle there's cling film in a draw. I check the fridge and there are covered salads and leftovers — this must be where they keep the leftovers for soldiers to eat. If we end up trapped in this building then it's nice to know we won't go hungry.

As I'm searching for the kitchen, I find a smaller office on the opposite side, away from the line of sight from the main courtyard. I request permission to move Rage in there so I can work on her. Dune agrees.

I'm alone with Rage, not wanting her to wake up and be embarrassed by a lot of people watching as I remove some of her clothes. I carefully cut away her top from her back, and this is the first time I see the scars. These are not the scars of battles lost and won; these are the scars of torture — precise cuttings, perfectly round burns. I hold her right hand up to the light and her fingernails are stunted and warped. I lay her hand back down, feeling guilty for seeing a part of her that I know she wouldn't willingly show me. I also know that I will never be able to fully understand Rage, because she is a child of war far more than I am or ever will be.

I strip off my t-shirt from underneath my jacket and cover her, and then I leave her burnt arm in the lukewarm water. Her eyes flutter every now and then; I hope she's not too severely concussed, that there hasn't been any damage. After ten minutes, she begins to stir.

"Hey, how's your head?"

"Broken." Her voice is weak and cracks.

"I need you to stay awake if you can." I get up and rummage around in the desk draws, finding a half-full blister pack of paracetamol tablets. I hand Rage two, and my canteen. She swallows them straight away.

"So what was that bomb called?"

"Which one?"

"The one that knocked you on your bum." She's squeezing her eyes shut tight and gritting her teeth and I don't want to ask what's hurting her more, her burnt arm or cracked head."

"Kitty."

"Kitty?"

"Looks all small and unassuming but will rip you apart if you get too close." I don't bite down on saying "like you did" but she says it for me, "Like I did."

"You can't always be right you know — it'll make you insufferable and terribly unlikeable," I chastise.

"You have a terrible bedside manner."

"Sorry." I look at my watch, her arm's been in water for nearly twenty minutes, but I want to leave it in a little longer as I wasn't able to get it in immediately.

"Cass, I need you to be honest with me."

"Sure."

"Are those bits of cloth permanently sealed to my arm? I mean if they are, fine, but you know, I'd prefer not…"

"No, we'll get a doctor to remove them. I can't do it though, I'll cause way more damage."

"Are we trapped?"

"Yeah, we're trapped."

"There's a mole."

"Yeah, there must be." I let out a weary sigh. Another mole.

I gently remove Rage's arm from the water and very carefully pat it dry with her ruined top. She flinches and hisses at me but doesn't scream, which is incredibly impressive considering the agony she must be in. I carefully wrap her arm in cling film and let her rest a little while longer.

"Who do you think it is?"

"The spy?"

"Yeah."

"Someone on this mission. The other teams didn't know our plans in full. It seems the most likely answer."

"I agree." She looks thoughtful and I wonder who she believes to be the culprit. There's a small smile on her face and her head is tilted slightly to her right, and that's when I realise she must be talking to Night.

"He's going to look into it," she says, as she opens her eyes to look directly at me.

"Ready to re-join the others?"

"Sure. I'm not going to be able to use a rifle — I'll need a small side arm instead." I'm taken aback momentarily until I remember that it's Rage who's talking. I go back to the desk, pull out a gun, and load it for her.

"You were going to leave that in here?" Rage looks at me with disgust.

I ignore her derision and lead the way back to the others.

Yve and Luca are standing either side of the window with the blinds down and their rifles loaded and ready. Ellyas is talking with Dune and Echo.

"We can't get back to our truck out front and our only chance is a vehicle of some sort." Dune taps the table to indicate where our truck is parked.

"The garages are back here." Ellyas moves a stapler to a random location on the desk.

"Where are we?" I ask, and he points to the book.

"And the paperclips are the soldiers?" There are paperclips scattered in front of the book.

"Yeah."

"How many around the back?" I ask.

Dune responds, "We're estimating fifteen, each paperclip signifies five soldiers." He places three at the rear of the building.

"There are thirty out front?" They all nod.

"Our odds aren't good." Echo rubs her temple in concentration. Rage narrows her eyes at her.

From the window Luca says to me, "And don't even think about suggesting the roof, Cass." He glances over to me, smiles, and then focuses back on his duty.

I smile back. "Not this time." I look at Rage. "Any more toys left?"

"Just one." She pulls it from her pocket and it's not one of hers, it's manufactured.

"Where did you find that?" Echo asks.

"When I was sneaking around planting my own bombs." She doesn't hide the pride in her voice.

"What does it do?" I ask.

Dune takes it from her. "It's a next-gen flash grenade. Smaller, more powerful." He grins. "Okay guys, you're going to need to memorise our route because we'll be doing this practically from memory. We wait out the flash and go, but we will still be temporarily blinded." There's a spark in him I haven't seen before; this must be him truly in action. Echo smiles with her perfectly painted red lips, but she's wincing slightly as she re-ties her ponytail. Rage watches her.

We make our way to an opposite office and we can hear the troops outside — it's likely they're about to storm the building. "Now or never!" Dune yells.

Each of us has taken a turn looking through a crack in the blinds to visualise our route. Running a gauntlet partially blinded by the flash bomb has to be the stupidest thing I've ever thought of doing whilst men with guns want to kill me. At least, I think it is; it's hard to keep track at this point. We already have our earplugs in. It's surprising how often you need them when you're a soldier, and we all have them stored in our top pockets. Luckily, I'd managed to salvage Rage's before I ditched her top.

Using the butt of his rifle, Ellyas smashes the window and steps back, and Echo brushes down the shards from the frame with the end of hers. She moves out of the way and we cover our eyes as Luca finally gets to show off his athletic prowess and the arm that had so many universities interested in offering him a scholarship. The flash bomb drops and erupts. For the initial impact, we stay back, eyes shut — the first blast is too strong for us not to be affected if we were out there. After ten seconds, we move.

The new type of flash bomb lasts longer — my ears are ringing horribly as I barrel through the window. I can just about make out the shouts of soldiers running from the front of the building towards us and being hit with the flashes from the stun grenade. Luca, Ellyas, Echo, and I run full tilt, just about making out our path through our partial blindness. The flash fades when we're metres from the barracks that block our path to the vehicles; blotches of whiteness still impair my vision. The soldiers are starting to clear their heads; we only have seconds. There's a loud explosion from the front of the building and Dune, Yve, and Rage come running around the side. I don't know how she's moving so fast considering her injuries, and I really don't know how she can have a smile on her face at a time like this, but she does.

The barracks are still locked thanks to our earlier manoeuvre, but some of the windows have been broken and soldiers are now jumping out of them. I fire my ES gun at one approaching to my right, re-holster it, and pull out my handgun; I kneecap an approaching soldier with a single bullet that would have shattered the bone. He screams and the sound is chilling. Echo silences another approaching soldier with a bullet to the head, and Luca's bullet tears through another's just beneath their collarbone. We keep moving round the barracks and finally have the garage in our sites.

"We'll cover you both, get us a jeep." Ellyas indicates to Echo and me as he and Luca raise their rifles. There are soldiers approaching from either side but we don't hesitate. We duck as we run. This is our only chance. There's another explosion and I have no idea how Rage is doing it. A bullet grazes my upper arm; I'm able to ignore the sting of it as we finally reach the door. It's electronically locked and the doors are large and re-enforced. Echo swears under her breath.

"Your ES charged?" I ask her.

"Yeah."

I pull it from its holster in her belt, step back, and fire it at the electronic keyboard, frying it. Sparks fly and then we hear the distinct "click" of the doors unlocking.

"Wasn't sure that'd work," I say, as I hand back her device.

"I'm pretty sure it shouldn't have," Echo utters as she pushes one of the vast doors aside just enough for us to slip inside.

The room reminds me of going to see a war exhibit at school where they had an auditorium filled with old army vehicles. There are so many for us to choose from. We find the keys and we're searching for the corresponding number plate to the keyring when Luca and Ellyas fly into the room with Dune, Yve, and Rage right behind them.

"What are you guys doing?" I'm surprised they risked running across the open space to reach us.

"There's too many of them, we didn't have a chance of holding them off," Luca replies.

"Please don't tell me we're trapped again." Rage just shrugs at me and strolls casually towards the tank Echo and I were about to test drive.

"I see you learned a thing or two from me." Yve nods her head towards where I'd ES'd the keypad, reminding me of the time we broke into a medical supply warehouse to get vital medication for my mum.

"I definitely added more finesse," I smile back.

"We need a plan — the tank alone may not cut it." Dune strides over to the tank and pats it on the muzzle of its gun. I can tell Rage is thinking what I'm thinking when she glances at the rows of keys and then, from the corner of my eye, I see Echo absently rub her temple.

"Are you okay, do you need some painkillers?" I go to pull out the ones I had taken from the office in case Rage needed more.

"That old tech's a real bitch, isn't it?" Rage crosses her arms as she addresses Echo.

"Rage?" My stomach clenches. Is she implying what I think she's implying? Echo's hand has frozen midway to dropping to her side.

"What are you talking about?" Echo is trying to sound casual but I can see the tension.

"The tech — duh. The first implant was a right nightmare. Whenever you'd get sent a message or sent one out it was like a punch to the temple. That's why they upgraded us to the newer model." Rage runs her finger along the scar behind her ear. "But part of the problem was the placement of the old model." Rage pulls back her hair near her left temple to reveal a small scar.

I step back from Echo and raise my gun. "Put your weapon down."

"Woah! What are you doing, Fortis?!" Dune demands.

"She's your mole," Rage states as she also brings her gun up. Luca and Ellyas follow suit.

"Don't be ridiculous, I just have a headache, but this little shit has just shown her hand. So it was you who revealed our plans and let us walk into a trap?" Echo brings up her rifle and aims it at Rage.

"Rae, she has a point. You've just shown us you're a spy." Dune still hasn't touched his weapons.

Rage rolls her eyes. "I'm a double agent *Nick*."

"It's true, she's been helping us," I admit to him, and his expression turns dark.

"What have I told you about following the chain of command?"

"Sir, I apologise, but right now, we need to address the real issue — Echo is our mole."

"You have no proof." He looks around at us all as though we've gone mad.

"She worked for the GDO for years," I counter.

"I was betrayed," Echo spits.

"Were you betrayed by your girlfriend or turned?" I ask and look her in the eyes, and Dune sees it then, the truth, because she can't hide it. She was turned.

"You? You were the one who betrayed us?" Dune asks horrified, heartbreak written on his face.

"I did it for love," she replies, her chin held high, her gun still pointing at Rage's face.

"Love? Screw love, Echo!" Dune shouts. "Freedom of our people is more important than love. Love is trivial; you do not let thousands die for love!" He looks around at the room we're trapped in and holds up his arms in disbelief. "This isn't some poetic fantasy, this is war, this is death, and the future of those children in Naevena whose eyes you looked into and promised to save when you helped me pull them out of the wreckage of their school. You have killed them all, killed us all, all for your selfish ideal of love."

Echo looks at him and doesn't cry or plead; she stands firm, believing love is greater than freedom. Oh, how wrong she is. Love does not betray and love does not damn nations to tyranny, children to torture, families to starvation.

I take in Echo in all her selfishness; I turn from her disgusted and fearful. This could be it, the end of the Resistance. We're trapped, we have a traitor high up within our ranks, possibly one of many, our reinforcements have had to pull back and disperse. We are fighting an unwinnable war; I feel my hope being to vaporise.

And then I hear the shot. I spin back around and Dune has embedded a single bullet in her skull. She falls to the floor, dead. He takes a breath, choosing freedom over his love for her and speaks. "We need a new plan." Rage looks at him with swelling respect; I don't believe anyone has ever exceeded her expectations, except maybe for Night.

Rage nods at me. "We have an idea."

Dune stares at Rage, pointedly not looking at the body by his feet. "And you and I are going to have a very, very long conversation when we get out of here."

As I turn, I glance at Echo's body, her red hair splayed out around her, pooled in her own blood. I step over her and throw Rage the steering wheel lock keys for the number plates she calls out. We need to move quickly; Echo's revelation has delayed us too long. We need to put her to the back of our minds.

"Shotgun the Wolfhound!" Rage shouts as she runs towards the camouflage-painted, six-wheeled and caged vehicle.

"I'm driving," Ellyas barks at her, and then runs for the protected patrol vehicle when he sees her opening the driver's door. Yve follows reluctantly, knowing she'll have to somehow keep Rage in line.

Dune starts up the tank by turning on the master power switch. He moves it out to the front whilst Luca and I prep a few other vehicles. Rage peeks her head out of the Wolfhound.

"There aren't any big guns in here!" she shouts, and then climbs out, hoisting herself into the tank. I can't imagine what Dune is yelling at her, but he needs someone to work the gun for him, and Rage is, unsurprisingly, a good shot.

Luca lets out a whistle and I turn to see what he's just discovered.

"Can you drive it?"

"I mean, I gotta try, right? It's a great bit of kit."

"Can we get it out?"

Luca looks around. "Yep, once Dune gives the go ahead the path should be clear." I find the keys for any vehicles that are locked and throw them to him.

"I really hope you know how to drive it."

Dune gives the signal by letting Rage fire a shot from the tank's cannon through the front door. She turns, fires through the side door, turns, fires through the opposite wall. On the 'coms she yells out a stream of whoops.

Luca and I start up a couple of protected patrol vehicles, and using any heavy objects we can find we wedge the accelerators down, put them into gear, slam the accelerators to the floors, and get out quickly. We do the same with two more before making our way to the Stormer, a combat vehicle with a missile system.

"It's kind of cosy in here," I say, as Luca starts up the engine.

"Ready to roll?" Dune asks over the 'coms.

"We're ready," Luca replies, and then grimaces at me as he puts the huge vehicle into gear.

Dune starts the CR2 tank and drives through the blasted-open front doors, followed by Ellyas in his Wolfhound and us, a little further behind in our giant Stormer.

Outside there's chaos. GDO soldiers are firing on the trucks we sent out first, a few more are turning to fire on us, and two Husky vehicles are driving at full speed towards us. The CR2 tank's turret turns and fires on one of the smaller trucks — there isn't really any competition.

"Should we use our missiles or save them for later?" I ask Dune, semi-seriously.

"Save them, I think Rage would be offended if she wasn't the one to lay waste to this base."

"Why didn't you guys steal tanks before? They're so cool." Rage screams with glee down the radio.

"She's going to be far too hyped to sleep tonight," Luca tuts, and despite the fact we're surrounded by our enemy, that Dune just shot his girlfriend dead, that our mission failed, I laugh.

RAGE

"Can I fire on the barracks?" Rage looks through the sight on the turret. Her arm feels like it is burnt to the bone and her head is throbbing, but she was taught, long ago, to put her pain to one side.

"No," Dune replies, wearily.

The tank ploughs through the main gate into the compound and out towards Troyes.

"Wait, we're not going back to the farmhouse?"

"There's been a contingent plan since we moved into the farmhouse."

"What contingent plan?"

"The one where, if things completely fall apart, we relocate to a pre-chosen site."

"Where we going?"

"Somewhere safe. We were going to move there anyway before the final push to take Troyes."

"So… the GDO probably know about it then."

Dune sighs. "Probably, and seeing as it's a long drive, let's take this time to talk about the fact that you were, possibly still are, a spy for the enemy."

Rage feels, probably for the first time, uncomfortable. Dune has a point, which is awkward. She has betrayed them and he has every reason to suspect her of being involved in destroying their chance to take over the GDO base.

And he has just had to kill his girlfriend because she betrayed him.

"I'm sorry?" Rage replies.

"Why does it sound like you're asking a question about whether or not you're sorry?"

"Well, I was taken hostage by the GDO when I was six and forced to be a soldier for them, which involved killing likely innocent people and becoming an expert at making bombs by the age of eight, so you tell me why I'm not sure if I'm sorry." Rage realises that, after all, she doesn't feel that uncomfortable.

"Even so, and I am sorry for that, but you did feed information about us to the GDO."

"Yeah." Rage shrugs and takes aim at a nearby tree but decides not to decimate it.

"That's it?" She can see Dune is struggling to keep his temper under control.

"They are holding my best friend; if I do anything to displease them they'll torture him." The look Rage gives Dune is aggressive.

"Rae, I sympathise, but what you've done, it cost us a lot."

Rage thinks about this. She thinks about her friends, how Cassia was harmed by her actions. "I get that… but now my best friend is at risk because I chose to help you."

Dune lets out a sigh. "Rae, you're young, you've had a tough life so far, but you have to see this from my position. Allowing you to continue on missions with us is not possible. You have implanted technology that we can't track. How am I to know if you're leaking information because something has happened to your friend?"

"Then you need to rescue my friend."

Dune falls silent and Rage reconsiders decimating some trees. No matter what she does for the Resistance, they don't want to help her. If she isn't allowed to participate in missions then she may as well head back to the GDO base, and then maybe from there she can finally break out and take Knight with her. She is much more experienced now. She can make bombs from, well, just about anything. That's what she'll do. She'll rescue Knight on her own, and then the two of them won't be beholden to anyone.

KOHLER

Major Jay Kohler was not happy. The child they had embedded had been unable to feed in any useful information in days, and the operative they had working for years undercover had been found dead. Ambushing the Resistance on their raid would have made eliminating the cell incredibly easy. They'd found out all they needed through the moles they'd had infiltrate the camp. But they had escaped, and once again, Cassia Fortis and her friend were really, really starting to get on his nerves.

At least he still had Cassia. At least he was going to slowly wear her down until she decided to come for him, and then he'd finally be able to show her that he was in charge, that she is weak compared to him. She may have figured out how to limit her subconscious messages, but he'd break through the cracks. Oh, how he'd love to break through the cracks. And then he'd be the one to halt this foolish Resistance movement in its tracks.

The general entered his office as he was messaging her; he ended the conversation abruptly, giving his superior his full attention.

"What the hell happened? We had them! Then they just slip through our fingers with three of our vehicles — two of which are armoured fighting vehicles." He steps forward and slams both of his palms down on Kohler's desk. "Until now they've only managed to acquire combat trucks. How did you manage to mess this up so badly?" Kohler was showered in flecks of spittle as the general bellowed at him.

"Sir, the intel I had was faultless, but somehow they were able to outwit the men on the ground. I'm still trying to discover how."

"I just received a report — they say a child was on the scene, that the child was planting the bombs that caused the initial disruption, which led to their escape."

"Your operative did this?" Kohler got to his feet as anger bubbled up inside him.

"My operative? *My* operative?! I handed over this task force to you, Major. Under your command, it turned into a disaster. Clean this up." The general tapped his index finger down once onto the desk. "Clear?"

"Clear." The two men stared at each other, neither willing to back down, their matching ice blue eyes reflecting back the same expression. Major Kohler knew that rank had no standing in this moment. This was a battle of blood, of wills.

"See that every single one of them is destroyed. Including the operative. We've found, in the past, that using her Symbio partner is an incredibly effective disciplinary tool."

The general, his father, left and Kohler sat back down, opened his drawer, and poured himself a whisky. It was time for him to think of a new plan.

WEEK THIRTY

CASSIA

We arrive at the abandoned hotel under the cover of night. Unsurprisingly, military armoured fighting vehicles are incredibly uncomfortable for long journeys. I climb out feeling stiff and sore. Rage looks furious as she exits the tank, and Dune looks, well, withdrawn, but that's to be expected. I go after Rage to find out how her journey was, considering she chose to ride with the man who had threatened to find out the extent of her betrayal. I follow her to the doctor who has set up a makeshift triage in the foyer. I sit with her as he examines her arm and begins work debriding her wound. First he carefully washes her arm in saline, and then he puts numbing cream on her arm, apologising that he is out of morphine. Once her arm is numb, he slowly begins to cut away the pieces of cloth. I hold her other hand as she closes her eyes and looks away, not even bothering to try to pretend she's okay with this. I'm definitely not okay with it when I look up, and have to quickly look away as my stomach flip-flops. When he's finally finished removing the pieces of her top that had seared to her skin, he dresses her arm in a non-adhesive dressing and then another layer of bandaging.

"You're lucky I have any of this left." He goes into his bag and pulls out what he explains is some soft silicone to help protect her arm. When he's done, he gives me some pain medication to administer. Considering Rage is so young, I'm glad he's put me in charge of it.

Together we re-join the others inside the hotel dining room, where the rest of Sault and Unit 2 are waiting.

"Everyone accounted for?" Dune asks from behind me.

"All accounted for, boss," Ham says, although he's got a pretty severe scrape across his face and a lot of the others seem injured. Pranav is having his ankle strapped carefully by Drummer, and Jono is trying to clean a wound on Shreya's arm but she keeps batting him away. They all look a mess.

"Where's Echo?" Jono asks as he takes us in. None of us say anything; we're all waiting for Dune to speak but he takes his time.

"Echo was a traitor. She leaked all the details about our mission to the GDO, and without Rae's help we may not have uncovered her treachery until it was too late. Fortunately, this time, we all made it out relatively unharmed. We need to regroup and make a push for Troyes. A few more units will be joining us throughout the night. Ham, set up a watch."

And then he just leaves the hotel foyer and the rest of us are left standing around, feeling a little helpless and uncertain. As Ham begins to organise a rotation, Rage tries to sneak away, but I follow her.

"What's going on?"

She spins around, holding her injured arm against herself, and glares at me. "What's going on? You're never going to help me get Knight out of there, that's what's going on. I never should have believed you'd help me and now... now they're going to know what I did. Now they're going to hurt him to get to me."

"Rae, we're going to do everything we can to get him out safely."

"No you're not! You're going to go to Troyes and free it from the GDO. You don't care about him. None of you care about him, about us, about what they've done to us, about what they're doing to us."

"Of course we do, of course I do." She's frantic now and pushes me away when I reach out to her.

"No you don't! You have idea wha—" She stops and her eyes widen and she whispers, "No." She runs out of the room we've ended up in, through the foyer, and I chase after her. She jumps into one of the trucks and starts to hotwire it.

"What's going on?" Luca and Yve are standing in front of the hotel, watching us.

"Rae?" I say to her softly, but she keeps repeating "No" over and over and over.

And then she screams.

I have never heard a scream like it. She grasps her head, and I pull her out of the driver's seat and I'm surprised by her lightness. Sometimes I forget how little and young she is, because she's such a huge force. She's clutching her head and screaming as if her soul is being ripped from her body. I begin to sob because I know what's happening. Oh God, I *know*.

"What's happening to her?" Luca asks, next to me. He's watching her in fear, as is Yve.

"They have Night," I whisper, and they both look horror stricken as they understand that Rage is enduring his torture with him.

Luca carries her inside as she whimpers and claws at him, balled up in his arms. He takes her into an empty room, and I sit with her for the whole night, knowing that the entire time she's offering Night words of comfort, trying to pull some of the pain away. Neither of us sleeps, and then, as the sun rises, she freezes, her body so tense it must hurt.

"What is it?" I ask gently.

"Nothing."

"Nothing? It's stopped?"

"No." Her voice is taut, dead. "Nothing. There's nothing. No connection, just blackness. No string to pull. Nothing. Nothing." She then turns to look at me for the first time. "They killed him."

I go to hold her but she pulls away. "You did this."

"No, Rae."

"Don't call me that."

"Rage," I say pointedly, knowing that Night was the one who called her Rae. "*They* did this."

"But you could have stopped them."

"Not without a plan, not if we'd rushed in there immediately after trying to take the base."

"You did this." There's pure hatred in her eyes.

"No. Rage, the GDO did this. They did this." I take a risk; I reach for her hand. "Like they did this." I hold her small, damaged fingernails up. "This is what they do, to you, to him, to entire villages and towns. They destroy. They hurt us in ways that are beyond imagining. They did this."

She breaks down into tears, then, and eventually she lets me hold her. I feel like I've lost her, that she's already retreating into herself, into a dark place where no one can reach her. The place where Night used to be.

KOHLER

Kohler instructed his men to take the boy into a prison cell and beat him. He couldn't watch, and he knew he was a coward for not being able to watch. He began to sweat and his hands started to shake. And that's when he knew he had to stop it, stop them beating that small, frightened boy, the one who reminded him of who he once was. He marched into the room and put an end to it all. And then, when it was done, he went to the bathroom and vomited violently.

Why did it have to be children? He clutched the porcelain bowl. He shuddered. Anything else he could have endured. He flushed the toilet and washed his face, rinsed his mouth out. He must endure; he must, he thought. If not, then he had come so far for nothing.

RAGE

There's buzzing in her head. An emptiness crowded with the sound of an electric saw. It fills her head until she can taste the metal, smell the coppery scent of blood, feel the teeth bite into her flesh.

There's buzzing in her head and it's growing louder.

Buzzing.

Buzzing buzzing buzzing.

CASSIA

Around midday, Rage finally falls asleep. I walk down the hall and try to find Luca. He's sitting around a large table in what was once a conference room; Dune, Ham, Ian, a couple of people from Unit 5, and Yve are there as well. They're planning the push for Troyes. I'm so tired I feel slightly spaced out.

I sit down in a chair and listen to the planning, which washes over me even though I'm trying to take it in and form an opinion. Luca leans over to me and whispers.

"Go and lie down, you're not going to be much use like this."

"Oh, thanks," I grumble, but I let him lead me out of the meeting to our room, because I have no idea where it is. It has a double bed and an en suite bathroom. "This is ours?" I honestly can't believe the luxury of such privacy, even if the room is a little worn.

"Yep, and the sheets are clean."

"You're kidding?"

"Nope, everything was in a laundry cupboard in sealed plastic from the cleaners." I want to cry with joy — actual sheets that are clean and not old, mouldy, and dusty. "And, we have hot water too."

My bottom lip wobbles as he fills the bath for me — an actual bath with tiny little bottles of soap.

"What about Rae? Someone needs to watch her."

"I need to get back to the meeting but I'll ask Shreya for now and then take over myself."

"Thank you... I... Thank you." He kisses me, hands me a towel, and then shuts the door and leaves me to soak in perfumed bubbles. I can't believe I've found a slice of peace amidst the chaos and suffering.

Luca wakes me by climbing into bed next to me and wrapping an arm around me. I let out a sigh of contentment.

"You should get up otherwise you won't sleep tonight."

"How long have I slept?"

"About four hours." I still feel exhausted, but he's right, I need a full night's sleep if I'm going to be any use to our team. That doesn't mean I jump straight out of bed — I revel in this moment of privacy and normalcy for a short while longer.

Downstairs, the rest of the Resistance soldiers from the farmhouse are with us, having at least succeeded in their missions. It feels good to see so many familiar faces and a few more unfamiliar ones. They must be from the other Resistance cells that are joining us. Seeing this many people makes me think that maybe we're stronger than I thought, but a doubt niggles at me. There are too many of us in one place. Surely this makes us a target?

"Is Rae up?"

"No, Yve's in with her now," Luca reassures me. That makes me relax a little, that someone is keeping an eye on Rage. I don't want to think what this has done to her; I just have to hope that we can help her through her loss.

We make our way to what was once the hotel restaurant where the tables have been pushed together to create three long tables so we can all eat together. Luca and I sit with Jono, Ellyas, Drummer, Shreya, and Pranav.

"Do we have a plan?"

"Of sorts," Pranav responds as he passes me a jug of water. "Our intel shows that even though you guys were sent into a trap, the fact you got out and caused so much damage has effectively achieved our goal of taking down the base. We were able to contain the other two bases, and so that limits tactical support for Troyes. Across Old Europe there've been some other successes and failures. The Resistance has even managed to secure two air bases." I raise both my eyebrows at that; it's a first, and a big step forward. "We've been feeding in news of our victories, of Cassia Fortis, the girl who sparked a rebellion, now fighting to free Troyes." I feel incredibly uncomfortable with my infamy, thoroughly undeserving and, at the same time, deserving of the chaos I triggered. "And," he continues, "we've been using the tech from the implant to feed in false information, a little bit of misdirection."

"He does love some sleight of hand," Drummer grins, to which we all respond with a groan.

"So when do we move?" I ask, wary.

"Tomorrow," Shreya says without looking up from her plate of rations. Tomorrow? Tomorrow is far too soon. We're not prepared. We haven't laid enough groundwork. The reason the Resistance has made it this far is because it's been tactical, it's built up support, planned its movements. We wouldn't have such secure hideouts otherwise. This feels rushed, too impulsive. But Pranav tells me the order has come from outside our unit, others teams are ready to advance, and we have no choice but to give them our support.

"And how exactly are we to take the city?" I look around at my family, realising this could be the last time we're all together, because deep down I know what they're going to say. I can already guess what the plan is, and it's going to cost us.

After our meal, I go and check on Rage who is still sleeping. Yve looks weary beside her but tells me to get some rest as Jono has offered to watch her in a bit. I don't decline her generosity; I need a good night's sleep for tomorrow. Luca is already in our room when I walk in, and he approaches me as I shut the door and lock it behind me. We don't say anything; we don't have to — tonight could be the last night we spend together. We're not going to waste it.

I wake up in the morning having slept the entire night without a single nightmare. My Symbio implant lies on the bedside table next to me — there's no point in using it now. I've learned enough and don't have to cover for Rage anymore. I'm trying not to think about today, about what could happen to Luca, to my friends. I pull his arms around me tighter, wanting to feel the protection of them one last time. For as long as we can, we stay in bed, but too soon it's time to get up and face our enemy.

As we're dressing there's a knock on the door. It's Rage. I let her in and she immediately announces she's coming with us. I don't even try to argue with her but I do ask her for something. Dune wants to drum up as much support for our movement as he can, and he wants to use Rage as an example of what the GDO are doing to the children of Old Europe. Despite my hesitancy, she agrees. But she still seems muted to me, and I hate having to do this to her right now. I go downstairs with her. She's dressed in her Resistance uniform and so we make her change into GDO-issue clothing, and she stands next to the GDO Wolfhound we stole, rifle in hand, savage look on her face, as Dune takes her picture. He then sends it to all Resistance channels with a pre-written statement and instructions.

Rage practically rips the uniform off her body, puts on her Resistance clothing, and then turns to face me. "When do we leave?"

I turn to look at Dune for confirmation. "As soon as everyone is mobilised."

She nods once and climbs into the Stormer; Ham climbs in after her and gives me a reassuring look, followed by two members of Unit 5. I'm not even slightly surprised Rage has managed to get an invite into one of the assault vehicles.

My team is in the back of a truck together. Dune and Ian are in the tank, and Pranav has somehow managed to allocate himself as our driver. Drummer sits up front with him, and I'm glad they can be together for this. There's a nervous energy in the truck that I haven't felt before. We've been on missions — our last one was a big one, too — but this, this feels very different. There's a sense of impending disaster, maybe because we've lost some of our confidence after our recent tactical loss. Even Jono isn't trying to make a joke; in fact, he looks like he might vomit.

We finally set off, but my jittering nerves just make me feel unusually carsick. In fact, looking around everyone looks nauseated.

"Urgh, we need a distraction," I grunt.

"We so do," Yve concurs.

"I'm out," Jono manages to say through an unpleasant burp.

"Please don't leave it up to Luca to cheer everyone up," Ellyas exclaims.

"Hey!" Luca elbows him but it makes a few people smile a little.

"How about we place bets to see how long it takes before Jono hurls all over Yve?" I say, and Yve shunts away from him.

"But seriously, that might be soon. I think we need to pull over." We all start laughing until he starts retching and then we all yell at Pranav to pull over. Fortunately, Jono makes it out of the truck. When he's recovered we make him sit nearest the exit as we continue our journey.

"Remember when we met?" Yve says to me.

"In the back of a truck very similar to this."

"We were just simple thieves."

"Such small, obtainable goals."

"What happened to us?" I sigh as I adjust the strap on my rifle.

"We just got too ambitious."

"True."

"And you really pull off overalls." We laugh at our private joke — when we'd met at a GDO work camp, the overalls they'd given us were way too big. "Jake would have loved this."

I smile at that. "Yeah, he would definitely be saying ridiculous things to keep our spirits up." At least, I think he would have, because the Jake I knew before he died was very different from the one I'd grown up with.

"I was relying on Jono and Drummer to keep our spirits up." Yve looks at a grey Jono who just grunts in response.

"Oh, how times have changed when we are the ones to have to lift the team's spirits."

"Yeah, you're usually such a downer," Yve says to me.

I give her a look of severe derision. "You're the one who suggested eye spy."

"Hey, you can't knock the classics." Yve screws up her nose. "You know what, I'm actually looking forward to this. It feels like decisive action."

"Haven't our other missions been decisive enough?" Luca comments.

"Yeah, but… like, kinda small."

"You didn't get trapped in a GDO base."

"True, but still… this feels, meaningful. Assertive." She widens her pretty eyes.

"I agree." Shreya leans forward. "Until now we've just been an irritant to them, today we're really going to show them what we're made of."

"Hopefully not literally, like Jono." I grimace at him and he flicks me an angry glare.

Drummer turns around in his seat in the front. "Yeah, he always chunders before a big event, which is why it took him so long to have sex for the first time." Drummer grins at Jono. "Tell them about your first time mate, it's a great story."

"I hate you so much right now," Jono speaks through gritted teeth.

Drummer's face lights up. "So, his great and brilliant plan was a tactical chunder beforehand, and it worked, so that was all good. But what he didn't plan for was that the girl he was going to do it with, well, she was *a lot* more experienced, *a lot* and—"

"You know what, no one needs to know this story," Jono complains.

"Yes we do!" we all exclaim, but Drummer refuses to say any more, saying it is far more fun dangling the carrot. And it works, because we're no longer thinking about the danger ahead, we're trying to guess what horrendous thing happened to Jono the first time he had sex.

Pranav pulls over — we're at the outskirts of Troyes, and silence quickly falls over us as the reality sinks back in. It's mid-morning and it feels strange to be marching into a town without any real stealth. We all turn on our radios and look around at each other awkwardly.

"Do we put our hands in the middle or something?" Drummer jokes.

"Break?" Luca says with little commitment. We shoulder our packs and move out. Luca is heading up our team again; he is, without a doubt, the best choice — the most level headed of us, the most likely to actually follow Dune's orders, the only person we'll all actually listen to and not argue with. Basically, he's the only person adult enough to lead us without causing an argument.

We've been assigned to be part of the advance team; we're to enter the city and help protect the citizens, aiming for minimal loss of life. Pranav and Drummer will follow us in the truck as we walk ahead, giving assistance and reassurance. Clive and some of the Resistance intelligence network will have, by now, hacked into the GDO air force in Old France, disabled the drones, and interrupted the feeds for the jets. Our biggest threat isn't their ground troops but their air strikes. They would bomb the city with impunity with massive loss of civilian life. I've already seen burnt-out schools and hospitals, and I don't want to see any more; it is our responsibility to these people to free them and keep them safe at the same time. Resistance fighters have been inside Troyes for weeks now, secretly gaining support, ensuring that when the time comes for us to oppose the GDO we'll have the civilian's backing. That time is now; I just hope they've succeeded.

That's the plan, but plans fail.

RAGE

The rumble of the Stormer doesn't dim the sound of buzzing in Rage's brain, but she tries to drown it out by repeating over and over,

Rage rage rage
Until the mountains fall down

Rage rage rage
Until the mountains fall down

Rage rage rage
Until the mountains fall down

"You're only thirteen, right?" Ham asks her as he pulls over.

"Yes," Rage replies, her voice flat.

He tells her where to line up the missile launcher, and she fires — hell rains down on a GDO stronghold.

"Thirteen and you can do that…?" He sounds impressed.

She looks him directly in the eyes. "I am the sum of my actions." And Ham doesn't doubt her.

They move forward to assess the scene, but looking over the destruction Rage feels nothing, just her rage, her companion in the darkness, shrouding her from the hollowness in her heart.

CASSIA

Troyes already bears the wounds of war; empty spaces that may never be filled, ravaged buildings, and people already hiding, too aware of what's to come. It feels like a town haunted by spectres of its former residents, wraith-like and bruise-eyed. I thought we had filled them with hope, drummed up support for our cause, but that's not what I'm seeing. I'm seeing terror, and I feel like we're the invaders not the liberators. All these people want is to live without the fear of war hanging over them, and we've brought it right back to their doorsteps. I feel a sinking sensation in my stomach — guilt. Oh, that familiar guilt.

"Is that her?" I hear someone whisper from a doorway, and they're all looking at Yve, far more the poster child of a rebellion than I would ever be. I keep my eyes ahead and stay alert. We instruct people to go inside, stay away from their windows. We smile at children, we reassure. The rest of the Resistance is spreading through the city as we are, making sure not to give the GDO one large target to hit. Behind us, Resistance fighters are setting up blockades into the city, securing it for our victory.

As we approach Place de la Libération, we slow down. This is likely where we'll be ambushed. Jono steps forward with the metal detector for any mines we may trigger. Any other bombs they might use we just have to hope don't exist, because we don't have the tech on us to search for them. For the first time, as we move slowly, I take in this ancient city. It's breathtaking. The timber-framed buildings, all in different colours, leaning against one another for support, speak of a time long since passed but well remembered, well cared for. Here we are in the centre of it, trying to reclaim it, hoping not to create any of the destruction seen on the outskirts.

The metal detector goes off and Jono slowly crouches down; a metal trip wire runs along the ground. I crouch down next to him and tilt my head to the side, and the sunlight glints off the thin strands of metal. The entire square must be rigged. Jono speaks into his radio to tell all Resistance fighters that squares are likely to be set-up with trip wires and that the Place de la Libération is a no go. As we stand and assess what to do next, GDO soldiers approach from the opposite end of the square, treading purposefully and leading what must be a hundred innocent civilians.

"Oh, God," I breathe.

When they reach the centre, they move around more freely; there must only be wires around the perimeter. The soldiers force the people to their knees whilst we're all frantically thinking what we can do. What the hell can we do? We can't let these people be executed. We only have one choice. Luca radios in to Dune who sends further Resistance troops to the perimeter of the square.

Dune, over the radio, gives us our orders. We carefully step over the wire and keep low, make our way forward, and line up behind some shrubbery. We each take a knee and raise our rifles. This time I know I won't hesitate. Today, I am a soldier.

It feels as if time has slowed. I hear Shreya's slow exhale beside me. The glint of light off the rifle in a GDO soldier's hand draws my focus, the slight breeze shifting the fur on the hood of a kneeling woman's coat. We're waiting for their move; we cannot fire first with civilians being held hostage.

We wait, three breaths, four.

Then, a civilian is executed. The GDO soldier who pulls the trigger looks up and directly at us. It is a challenge. My heart feels like it's choking me as I watch the scene unfold as if in slow motion.

"Fire!" Luca shouts. We each have a soldier in our sights and we fire, as one, and so do the GDO soldiers, on us and on their hostages. We continue to return fire as the GDO slaughter the innocents they've rounded up. Each shot feels like a stone dropping into the pit of my stomach. I feel a bullet whip past my cheek and seconds after another hits

Shreya and she goes down. On instinct I crouch down over her — she's been hit in the left side of her neck and, oh God, there's so much blood. I stay bent over her as bullets scream past us, and I rip open one of the field dressings that I keep in my uniform. I place it over the wound and it immediately seals it and staunches the flow of blood, but where she's been hit, I don't know, she may not have much time. I begin to pull her out of the way and Pranav joins me whilst the others cover us by returning rapid fire at the enemy. We manage to lift her over the wire and drag her back down the road we came up and into a small side alley.

I put my hand on her cheek and look into her eyes. "I'm going to call for support. Pranav's here." She doesn't respond; I think she's too scared to talk. I call for assistance and then run back to the others. The others have dropped back to the street, hunched down with their backs to walls. We're less of a target now, but a lot of the hostages are dead.

"Head into the building." Luca motions to the empty gift shop on our right. As we make our way in, after Yve's smashed open the door, Jono is shot in the back of the calf. He falls down and we drag him the final couple of metres to relative safety.

"How did someone manage to hit your scrawny little leg?" Drummer asks as he dresses the wound.

"Beats me, I was running so fast."

I grab Drummer by the arm. "Pranav's in the alley with Shreya." And then I turn to Luca. "I need to go and help him."

I can see his reluctance when he agrees, but he still tells me to go and begins instructing the others to take up defensive positions, sending Ellyas to make sure no one's in the upstairs flat.

I find a back exit to the shop and make my way to the alley where Shreya and Pranav are.

"Have you heard from Dune?" Pranav asks me, his sister's blood now on his hands.

"They can't get the truck in, the GDO have us trapped inside the city." I look around and think; there must be a doctor's surgery nearby. I radio Luca and ask him to check his tablet, as I don't have mine on me. He radios back with directions and Pranav and I help Shreya stand. We're practically carrying her as we make our way down another side street, and then slowly and carefully down a more open one. We're taking a huge risk; an opposition soldier might see us. We see movement ahead and Pranav takes all Shreya's weight as I raise my rifle. He checks behind us as we stalk forward. When we reach the soldier, we see that he's slumped against the wall and breathing shallowly. I crouch down next to him and pull his field dressing from his pocket, where every soldier is taught to keep it, no matter what side you fight for.

"Hey!" he protests weakly. I look at him disapprovingly and lift his top to reveal his bleeding side. I carefully place the bandage over it and then swap places with Pranav. Taking Shreya's weight is a lot harder on my own but there's no way I could have supported the GDO soldier. We move even slower now and Shreya is barely conscious, but we round the corner and the doctor's surgery is two doors down. It is of course locked, but Pranav uses his knife to break open the old lock — we can hear voices inside and I call softly to whomever may be there. A frightened-looking nurse and female doctor appear wearing bloodied gloves.

"S'il vous plaît pouvez-vous nous aider?" I ask in my best recollection of French from school.

They look hesitant, but the doctor says, quietly, "Oui, oui, venez par ici." She takes off her gloves and helps me with Shreya; the nurse goes into a different room where I assume they are caring for another patient.

The doctor peels back the dressing and says to me, "Elle a besoin d'un hôpital." I don't really know how to respond to that. I know she needs a hospital, but how do I explain that I can't get her to one? She probably needs blood — I'd give her mine, but I have no idea what her blood type is. Pranav has helped the GDO soldier into a chair. I go to Pranav.

"I have to go and help the others. You need to stay here until we can get her out."

"Thanks, Cassia."

I turn and squeeze Shreya's hand. "I'll see you soon." She gives me a weak smile. I thank the doctor as I leave and make my way out to the street.

Being alone in a modern-day battlefield, I feel incredibly exposed. This may look like a normal town but there could be enemy soldiers anywhere. I head back the same way, not wanting to risk unknown side streets and getting lost. As I near the gift shop where the others are hiding out, brick dust explodes beside me. I instinctively duck as another shot is fired where my head was seconds before. I fire blindly in the direction of the shot and then run full pelt to the shop door. I make it inside with shell cases bouncing at my heels.

Luca gets up from his post and pulls me into a frantic hug. "I'm fine."

"How's Shreya?"

"She's with a doctor but she needs a hospital. What's the situation here?"

"We're at a standstill. They've killed thirty hostages and there are twenty-five of them still standing."

"Jesus."

"Ellyas managed to get the couple living upstairs out and into a building further away from the square, and now we're just waiting for our next move from Dune."

"Where is he?" I ask.

"Near the university — he managed to get the tank inside the city."

"We're going to need more than one tank." I sit down on the floor and look over at Jono. "How you holding up?"

"It's not been my best day." Drummer pats him on the shoulder and hands him a "Troyes" stick of rock.

Yve's standing by the window, keeping an eye on the square. "You know, I thought liberation would be more glorious and less, well, this." She points at the centre of the square where the GDO are dumping the bodies of civilians and soldiers into a pile, and by the looks of things, they intend to burn them.

"I really thought some of the GDO soldiers would defect to the Resistance." I feel completely at a loss. This wasn't the plan; we were supposed to have the support of the people. What has happened to the Resistance fighters who have been here for weeks? Have the GDO got to them first?

"Maybe they wanted to but were too scared," Luca says.

"It doesn't matter; you don't get to use the excuse that 'everyone else was doing it'. When something is wrong, it's wrong — there isn't a middle ground on this one. If they participate, they're guilty, whether they did it reluctantly or not."

"True," Drummer responds, "but we've been in the GDO, it takes a lot to stand up to them. Look at what Rage has done for them."

"She's only a child and they held her best friend against her. You saw what she endured." Drummer doesn't respond to me as I snap back at him.

"Cass, they're too scared to stand up to the GDO, you must understand that."

I glare at Luca. "The soldiers in that square are not scared of the GDO. I saw their faces, those soldiers are happy to be there, to be slaughtering innocents for 'the cause'. This, to them, is what *peace and prosperity* looks like. This, to them, is justice."

"Then we need to find a way to get through to them," Ellyas says as he examines the unfolding nightmare just outside the window.

And then I have an idea.

RAGE

Rage is frustrated being stuck in the Stormer with Ham and two soldiers she hasn't met before. They are completely out of the action, and what she needs right now is action. She needs to burn and annihilate. She needs to scream into the faces of these destroyers of children, to rip her way through the city and claim it back for Knight, for all the children she's seen harmed. For herself, for never getting to be a child, and for the scars that will never, ever heal.

"Rae, its Cass. I'm going to need your help." When Rage hears the plan, she smiles a smile of fury and retribution. The mountains *will* come down.

Rage tells Ham the plan and he leaves the other two soldiers in charge of the Stormer; Charlie and Benny, she thinks they're called. She doesn't really care.

"Do you have everything?" Ham asks her as they head into a residential area, cutting through back gardens to keep themselves hidden from view. The closer they get to the city centre, the harder it will be for them to find a route that isn't in full view of the GDO.

"Where the hell are all the Resistance fighters?" Rage whispers.

"Gone to ground whilst Dune re-groups. The GDO are using civilians as shields or hostages across the city."

"Urgh, such a dirty tactic. Why can't they just leave themselves open so I can shoot them all?"

"Because life isn't a video game, kid."

"Don't patronise me, Ham. I was killing Resistance fighters when I was eight years old. I figured out long before you did that life isn't a stupid video game."

"I keep forgetting what you've been through. I don't mean any disrespect by that, it's just, you are a kid. I wish you were actually a real one, for your sake."

"Yeah, me too." But in a way, she doesn't really.

"But, it's an honour to fight beside you, even if you're small and puny." Rage gives him a Rage look, which makes him smile. She guesses that maybe Ham isn't so bad. He speaks his mind, even if it annoys her, but at least he doesn't pretend with her, and she appreciates that.

"What's the plan now, then?" Rage says, as she watches a patrol of soldiers walk down the street near them.

"See that roundabout?"

"Pompidou?"

"Yeah, the one on Pompidou. It's not that pretty and it has three GDO trucks and zero civvies. Wanna throw something explosive at it?"

The smile Rage gives him this time is beatific.

Rage unzips her jacket and unclips a grenade. It isn't one of her own making, but it will do nicely. She creeps closer with Ham and hands him the bomb. Hiding behind an abandoned car next to a block of flats, Ham pulls out the pin and throws.

Rage tuts. "It's a little short."

"On purpose. How dare you doubt me." And he was right. The explosion throws the front vehicle backwards, knocking over a GDO soldier, destroying the second, and leaving the third for them to commandeer.

Rage climbs into the passenger seat of their newly acquired transportation. "Okay, your plan was pretty good."

"We needed wheels."

They drive up Boulevard Jules Guesde and pull over halfway up the canal.

"You sure about this?" Rage asks Ham.

"Worked like a charm before."

"I know but… won't we need it?"

"We need it now."

"I just think we should try to be more original and creative, like blow up the canal instead." Ham pauses and thinks about the idea for a moment.

"No, too many variables, we do the exploding driverless car thing again."

"Ugh, fine." Rage sets the car up and sends it on its way as she grumbles about Ham's lack of originality. "Um, I thought you said it would take twenty seconds to reach the square."

"It will… oh." The truck was going to overshoot the square.

"Well, it's a good thing I always keep a backup detonator." Then into her radio she says, "Get ready, Cass." She compresses the detonator and the truck flies into the air with the blast from the bomb.

Cassia and the others lay down cover fire as Rage and Ham race through the square and down the stairs into the underground car park. They run to the point they'd selected on the map, and Rage gaffer tapes the bomb Ham has been carrying to a pillar and sets the timer for ten minutes.

"We don't need that long."

"We don't know where our exit is."

"I'm assuming you have a backup detonator for this one, too."

"I'm not an amateur." Rage glowers at him and then runs to the opposite end of the underground space. "We came in the only exit... unless."

Ham looks around and sighs. "I'm on it."

He approaches the only 4x4 in the vicinity and breaks in, setting off the alarm. He unlocks the passenger door, and Rage jumps in next to him and finds and removes the alarm's fuse.

"And you didn't think we'd have an escape car." Ham tuts at her.

"Just hotwire the damn thing... Eight minutes." Ham pulls off the panel under the steering wheel and using his knife begins to strip back the wires.

"You are so slow at this... Seven minutes." Ham snorts at her and puts out his hand for the gaffer tape. Rage hands him a strip and he twists the wires together, starting the car, and then tapes them up.

"Six minutes, honestly, that's the slowest I've ever seen anyone start a car."

"Are you just going to criticise me constantly? If you are, I'll find a new partner." Rage grudgingly shuts up because she quite likes the idea of being Ham's partner. The huge, brown-haired, bearded man who was built as if he'd consumed a pig a day since childhood and it had converted to muscle, not fat, was a pretty cool partner to have.

"We should leave just before the bomb detonates; we're less likely to get shot."

"But more likely to be crushed under debris."

"I hope that doesn't happen, because if it does we totally failed." Rage talks into her radio, "Cass, you have five minutes. Start moving." She turns to Ham. "Are you sure I shouldn't drive?"

"Kid, your feet don't reach the pedals. I hope you have a strong stomach." He grins at her wickedly and the buzzing fades a little as her adrenaline begins to build.

CASSIA

Drummer and Jono are on the first floor, having helped give cover fire for Rage and Ham as they sprinted into the underground car park.

"Are you ready for this?" Luca asks me, and I honestly don't know the answer. I'm scared, of course I'm scared, but we came here for the people of Troyes, to start making a difference. I have to believe that we can do this, that it was worth going down this route. But I can't stop thinking of alternative ways we could be fighting them. The GDO have to be stretched too thin, as there aren't that many soldiers in this city; how can they keep an eye on all of Old Europe successfully? But, even though I want to find a different route to our end goal, I know that right here, right now, my role is set.

"I'm ready." I kiss Luca once, quickly, and hear Rage announce that we have thirty seconds. I stand by the door with my best friend and my boyfriend at either side of me and take a long, deep breath. The other Resistance soldiers nearby announce that they're in position. Yve briefly squeezes my hand.

We hear and feel it before we see it. The bang of an explosion is unmistakable and the ground beneath our feet shudders. I see the entire world around us tilt to one side and then right itself. Only then do we see the ground begin to collapse in the far corner opposite us and a car flying through the exit of the car park.

"Now!" Luca yells into our radios. We sprint through the door, Jono and Drummer giving us cover fire, Ellyas and Yve right behind us. The ground trembles again, more violently, and we stop and brace ourselves, the civilians and soldiers in the centre of the square panicking as the ground begins to crack and collapse. We start moving again, Resistance soldiers from all sides running to the centre, rifles and firearms aimed at us. A GDO soldier turns to face us, but Luca lifts his gun and shoots him, and the man falls instantly. The civilians are screaming and trying to run whilst the GDO soldiers are trying to hold them back. A soldier has a woman in a headlock. I think quickly — my ES gun will likely send the electroshock into her body as well, and I'm too close to use my gun and not risk collateral damage. Instead, I whip my handgun across his temple — even if it doesn't bring him down it's going to really, really hurt. I block out the chaos around me as the soldier staggers and loosens his grip. I rip the woman from his arms and point to the canal.

"Run," I instruct. I wheel around and knee the same soldier, who is bent over, in the nose. He collapses, hands over his face, blood spraying between his fingers. Yve is fighting hand-to-hand with another GDO female soldier, her eyes filled with wrathful fire, and I know she doesn't need my help. Luca is helping up a couple of civilians, and I don't have to yell at them to run, which they're instinctively trying to do anyway; they run towards where Rage and Ham are waiting, and where Dune's re-enforcements are approaching from.

I'm grabbed by the arm; I twist around to face my assailant and they wrench on my arm and I scream out in pain as my shoulder is torn from its socket. I'm furious, and so I kick the man, who is twice the size of me, right in his manhood. He doubles over, retching, and using my one good arm I fire my ES gun on him as added punishment.

My right arm is now useless, and being right-handed I'm at a severe disadvantage. Only about half the people have escaped, and the ground is starting to tilt beneath our feet. I re-holster my ES gun onto my right hip and, holding my handgun in my left hand, I run towards the nearest GDO soldier, cradling my right arm with my other hand, gun still securely grasped in it. The soldier turns to me and I see his fear and indecision. I raise my gun and yell at him to drop his weapon. He throws his rifle to the ground at my feet. "Now run," I say, low and just loud enough so only he can hear. He runs in the same direction as the hostages. The rifle is useless to me, but I pick it up anyway, not wanting it to be used on one of us by an enemy soldier. There's only a small group of civilians left in front of us, about ten or so, but there are six GDO soldiers, all fully armed, and they don't look like they plan to move for anyone. I see Luca charge at one of them, but he can't see the soldier behind take aim at him. I yell for him to move, and without really thinking about it I raise my left arm and shoot at the soldier. The bullet rips right through his neck. Luca manages to control his surprise as he floors the soldier in front of him and knocks him unconscious with two swift punches to his face.

Yve is now beside me, panting and covered in blood — I can't tell if it's hers or not. Two shots are fired from the direction of the canal and two GDO soldiers go down. Ham and Rage remain poised to fire again at the other side of the square. The ground shifts once more and we yell at everyone to move. The rest of the Resistance fighters begin to run, along with the remaining GDO soldiers and hostages. Luca, Ellyas, Yve, and I almost make it to the other side when the ground begins to tilt dramatically, and without warning we're running uphill, forcing ourselves to climb the collapsing ground. My arm is in agony but I keep pushing forward. Ellyas gets there first and leaps up onto the ledge. Yve's in front of me and scrambles up the lip of the concrete ledge now jutting out horizontally above us and Ellyas hauls her over the last bit. Using my good arm, I push her upwards as Ham grabs her arms and pulls.

Luca yells at me to go first, but I don't know how I'm going to haul myself up with one arm. He lifts me by the waist, but there's a loud rumble and the ledge we're on shifts and we slide further down.

"You need to put my arm back in its socket. I'm useless without it."

"I've never done it before." Luca looks terrified.

"Try. Please." He grabs my arm by the wrist and elbow and quickly assesses movement, which I don't enjoy. I lie down, worried that if I faint I'll knock myself out and then we'll be trapped in this pit.

"I saw one of my team mates getting their shoulder put back in... I hope this works. If not, please still love me afterwards."

"I'll do my best." I close my eyes and he slowly but firmly pulls on my arm at an angle, and then I hear the grinding clunk of my shoulder slotting back into its socket. I grit my teeth through the pain.

"You okay?"

"I love you a little less, but yeah, better." I allow myself two seconds of rest before getting up. "Thank you."

The slab we're on has begun to crack. "Cass, we have to move." He pushes me ahead of him as the world tilts and I clamber awkwardly up to the ledge where Ham is now hanging his arms down to me, Ellyas anchoring his legs. I grasp his wrists and yell out in pain as he helps to lift me; my shoulder feels like it's tearing itself out of its socket again, but as I land clumsily on the tarmac I realise it hasn't popped out. I quickly turn around to see Luca pushing himself up onto the ledge and swinging his legs up and over. Relieved, I look back to see a group of dusty, frightened-looking people. The Resistance fighters have the GDO soldiers kneeling with their hands tied behind their backs. Rage is one of the people holding them at gunpoint.

As I stand, I see a familiar tank approaching, followed by three protected patrol vehicles. Dune climbs out of the tank and approaches us.

"We need to get these people in the trucks, they'll take them to the hospital — we've secured the building, they'll be safe there." We begin helping the injured into the vehicles. I instruct a man who looks to be in his thirties to get into a truck but he refuses. I'm too tired at this point to attempt any

French and I look around helplessly. Dune approaches and speaks with him.

"What is it?" I ask.

"He wants to stay and fight."

"He does?" I look at the man, not able to comprehend why anyone would choose this moment to join the fight after witnessing so many losses.

"He says that he thinks some of the ones who weren't injured might want to as well." I look around and I see something in their eyes — anger, and the desire to finally do something about it. I understand that desire, and I feel that same need, to fix what's so broken about our society.

We see the trucks off, and eight men and two women stay behind with us, plus the tank.

"What the plan?" Yve asks Dune, her chin raised, her eyes clear and focused.

"We're still going to take back this city and we're doing it today." Dune begins to deliver his instructions.

Throughout the city there are around a hundred Resistance fighters, around eighty thousand inhabitants, and three hundred GDO soldiers. The numbers are on our side if we can show people that they need to fight for their beliefs once again, that it's okay to stand up for what you believe in, that they have a right to speak, to disagree, to want change. And so we do something that hasn't been seen since the first year the GDO took over. We stage a protest.

With the GDO throughout the city beaten, we go from door to door, protecting the civilians who have joined us. They bring people out of their homes and businesses and onto the streets. Soon there are three hundred of us walking the streets, and the inhabitants are chanting, chanting that they want to take back their city, take back what's theirs. More of the Resistance fighters join us as we lead the march, protecting the growing crowd of people. As their voices rise as one, I feel my hope swelling with them and I know that this is the right way to fight this war. To rise up and refuse to accept the oppressive regime that was forced upon us. To stand together.

The streets fill with people, and they're mourning their loved ones recently lost and those taken long ago. They have answered our call, and finally, the Resistance has its movement, finally it can make a difference.

By the time darkness falls, we have reclaimed Troyes for its people.

On our way out, we stop by the hospital to see Jono, whom Drummer helped into the trucks with the hostages, and to see how Shreya is doing. She's in ICU and we can't go in to see her; Pranav tells us she lost a lot of blood and then breaks down crying. Drummer holds him as we wait.

Waiting to see how Shreya is feels as though we're not contributing, all of us still high on emotions we don't know what to do with, and so we assume guard duty at the hospital, not wanting to leave until we have news of her. It keeps us here and gives us something to focus on. I'm patrolling the main perimeter with Dune when I ask him what will happen with Paris, our main target.

"We'll go back to the hotel and begin planning. We need to keep the momentum up though — with this anti-GDO sentiment finally bubbling to the surface, we have a real chance."

"Paris won't be as easy."

"No, it won't, but it's a step forward. We're making progress."

"And the children?"

"I've been thinking about them ever since I spoke with Rae. I don't want to consider Paris until we've stopped what the GDO is doing there. We can't allow such a practice to continue."

"I'm glad you said that." I smile at him and I feel a small sense of relief. Rage needs this; she needs to go back there with us and put an end to that nightmare of a place. But I need it, too. Ever since I found out what the GDO were doing to children, I've had this restless desire to stop them, a desire even stronger than my need to fight them.

WEEK THIRTY-ONE

RAGE

Rage is on watch with Ham at the third floor reception of the hospital when Cassia comes to see them. Cassia's face is drawn and they both know what it means.

"She didn't make it?" Rage asks, her stomach dropping.

"No." Cassia's voice is thick with emotion. No one says anything; they've all suffered the loss.

"How's Pranav?" Ham asks.

"Drummer's with him." Cassia takes a deep breath, fighting her grief. "But I do have some good news." Rage looks at her questioningly. "We're going to your base, Rae, and we're going to free the kids."

"And we're going to make them all pay." Rage's voice is flat and cold.

"We all will," Ham responds, and puts his huge hand on Rage's small shoulder.

KOHLER

Major Jay Kohler dismissed the captain in his office who was introducing him to their newest recruit, a snivelling eight-year-old who stank of filth. He resented his position once more, a babysitter to these children — it was an insult really. He could see that now. With Fortis no longer linked to him, the fun really had left the game. He needed to be posted to Utonia; it was the only way he'd get where he needed to be. Then his father would be proven wrong.

He went to what he called the war room and examined the map of GDO territory. It was there that he heard reports of events unfolding in Troyes, and that was the first time he saw an image of the operative who betrayed the cause and became a double agent. It was a poster sent virally through Resistance channels, which they monitored constantly. It was of a young mixed-race girl, with black hair, dark blue eyes, and her head tilted downwards, but she is looking directly at the camera and there's a rifle on her shoulder. The text reads:

THE GDO'S NEWEST RECRUIT
It's time to say NO to the GDO

So they made it rhyme. So what? The GDO were stronger than a stupid little poster, Kohler mused as he dismissed the findings. Propaganda no longer had a place in this war; that time had long since passed. Now was a time for action, and he was planning on taking some serious action.

CASSIA

I'm sitting alone in a plastic chair; the loss of Shreya still hasn't sunk in and I can't seem to get myself to move. I know we'd never been close, but we were finally beginning to work things out. I can't help thinking who else we're going to lose in this war — first Jake, then Night, now Shreya. What if we lose another member of our team? What if I lose Luca?

My head is aching and my eyes feel dry as I sit in the waiting room, my coffee now cold and stale in my hands. Through my numbness, a painfully familiar sound causes me to stand. I feel my breathing slow, and I wait, hoping that maybe my tired mind has conjured the rush of engines tearing through the sky. The sickening noise that follows confirms what I feared.

The GDO are bombing Troyes.

We didn't win. We didn't change anything.

Kohler was right.

Around me, I notice every other GDO soldier is standing, frozen in place — all those people who stood beside us, who believed that we were going to instigate change, that the GDO weren't a threat to them. My eyes close slowly and the image of scores of hopeful, innocent people walking as one against their oppressor down ancient, beautiful streets scorches itself against my eyelids. I'd thought the worst of this day was done: the loss of one of our own, the loss of the civilians in the square, the others throughout the city who were used as a means of displaying the hold the GDO still had over us. I was hideously mistaken. Their worst is beyond imagining.

I don't know how long I stand there.

Yve joins me later with her own cup of awful coffee. We sit there, watching the nurses and doctors going about their work in silence. My arm is now in a sling, one of the doctors having checked it over earlier.

"You know what? War's a bitch." Yve keeps her eyes ahead as she speaks. There's no humour in her voice.

"Total bitch." It's all we know how to say about what's happened. It's all we can say. The pain, the guilt, the regret are all too great to put into words, and so we sit, knowing that our actions have killed thousands. It's not something you can reconcile. It's not something that we'll ever recover from. Our souls will forever be marred with the lives we helped take today. We are just as responsible as the GDO, because we weren't prepared for this fight, and we both know it.

We sit together quietly, neither of us drinking but holding onto our paper cups nonetheless.

Softly, Yve says, "I feel bad for not knowing her better."

"I feel bad for not liking her better."

We sit in silence again and I think of Shreya. She was passionate, loyal to our cause, loved by her brother and yes, by us. Despite the fact we weren't really friends, we would have done anything for her; I would have, as we would for any one of us.

"I can't imagine what Pranav is going through," I say.

"Yes you can." Yve turns to look at me and I remember Jake, my best friend, her boyfriend. He wasn't my brother but we'd been inseparable most of our lives and I had loved him. I still love him.

"Yes, I can." I rest my head on Yve's shoulder and let out a sigh. "I'm so tired it hurts."

"Me too."

Ham walks through the waiting room, spots us, and walks over. "Soldiers." I lift my head off Yve's shoulder and we greet him back.

"Are we heading out soon?" I ask, wanting to leave this place, wanting to turn my back on this pain, this loss that's too big, too awful to take in.

"Yeah, that's why I came to find you. Now the bombing has stopped it should be clear to leave. It'll be a difficult journey though."

"What have you done with Rae?" I look around, concerned.

"I haven't done anything with her — I don't think anyone can control that little terror. She's pestering Dune about something." Ham has a look on his face that tells me he's come to like her, probably respect her as well, seeing as he fought alongside her.

"We'd better go before Dune loses his mind." I get up, worried Rage is about to get herself court-martialled, relieved to have something else to focus my mind on.

Back at the hotel, Pranav slips away to his room and Drummer lets him go, giving him his space to grieve. Despite being exhausted, we all head to the old restaurant and sit down, talking quietly until Dune enters. We fall silent as he takes his place at one end of the room.

"Today we lost friends, siblings, loved ones." He pauses. "Nineteen of us." He lists every single person's name and we bow our heads and remember them, honour them. After a moment of silence, he continues. "But we lost more than just that." For the first time ever I see Dune struggle with words. "There will be setbacks along the way, there will be a great many losses, but we must endure, we must continue to believe in what we're fighting for."

He takes a moment to collect himself. My heart is hammering so hard from our dereliction of duty — we had promised the people of Troyes we would save them. Instead, we led them to their execution. There is no penance to make up for what happened. And I knew what would happen; I have seen it before, in Auria, in the towns we had seen burnt down. The GDO always retaliates a thousand-fold. We should have known. We should have been prepared and protected the people we'd sworn to save. We failed. We failed abominably.

"This is how the GDO operates. They want to instil so much fear that we won't fight for our freedom, but we must. We are the only hope left in Old France, in all of Old Europe. We cannot allow our lives, the people of these nations, to be dictated to by a despotic regime." He pauses, and I can see his hands shaking.

"Tomorrow we will fight a new battle." His voice has become thick. He clears his throat and nods towards Rage. "As you may know by now, Rage was taken by the GDO when she was only six years old, and she was forced to train as a soldier, forced to kill for them." There are murmurs about the room; some didn't know, and I'm worried how they'll react to her at this news, but Dune continues, not allowing them to voice any suspicions about her.

"There are other children, like Rage, who are being subjected to this unimaginable cruelty — they are being tortured, pushed beyond what most adults can endure. These are the children of our nations. They should be protected and cherished, not bullied and beaten." I can feel everyone in the room stirring; the atmosphere is changing. Our losses combined and our anger at this injustice is rising up, giving us fuel for the fight ahead.

"We will take Paris but before we do, we will right this wrong, we will free these children, and we will not let the GDO take any more from any of us!" His voice rises to a shout and his eyes glisten with unshed sorrow. We all holler and cheer with him. Rage sits silently and looks around, and there is a fierceness in her expression that makes me worried we've lost her. Too much has been taken from her for her to find her way back; the child inside might truly be gone.

Carl brings out some food for us, and I see Rage get up and help him and I reconsider my earlier assessment. Maybe she hasn't slipped too far from us. I get up and help her, not speaking, but I can feel her looking at me every now and then, and when I sit down to eat she sits next to me. Ham comes and joins us, and then Yve, Jono, Drummer, Ellyas, and Luca, and finally, Dune.

"Jeez, Rae, did the GDO not teach you table manners?" Jono asks.

She looks up at him and I'm terrified for a moment about how she'll react to the joke that was, typically, in poor taste. "They said to spear your food like it's a Resistance fighter." She stabs her knife into a slice of cold beef and Ham lets out a bellowing laugh, which sets all of us off. Rage tears off a piece of beef with her teeth and grins maniacally at Jono.

"Where is this base anyway?" Drummer asks.

"South of the farmhouse, near Lyon."

"You know, I miss the farmhouse," Jono says. "I know the beds were rubbish and we didn't have our own en suite, but I still miss it."

"You just miss sharing a room with all of us," Yve observes. "It's because you're scared of the dark, isn't it?"

"I'm sure I'd feel better if you shared my room with me tonight." His smile is sweet as he replies.

"Well, that is *quite* the offer... How could I refuse?" Yve beams at him. Jono is too surprised to retort, which makes all of us laugh, even Drummer. We spend the rest of the meal joking with each other, like we usually do, and it feels like a balm after recent events. When we've finished and have helped clear up, we all head to our rooms. I'm worried about Rage being alone, but I hear Yve asking her if she wants to hang out for a bit. Rage accepts the offer and I'm relieved that she won't be by herself.

The following morning I head to Yve's room and knock gently on the door. Yve opens it, and she's clearly only just woken up yet somehow looks like she's doing a photoshoot where the theme is "sensual sleepy". I can't help but resent her a little for it.

"She's still asleep." Rage is curled up under the covers at the edge of the bed, breathing softly.

"Thank you for taking care of her last night."

"Well, it's not like I had a man to keep me company." She winks at me but I can feel the sadness behind her words.

"At least she doesn't snore."

"That's so true… She does kick though." Yve pulls down her tracksuit bottoms to reveal a bruise the size of a twelve- or thirteen-year-old's heel on her thigh.

"Ouch… Wait, are you sure that's not from yesterday?"

"She doesn't need to know that." Yve lifts her chin primly.

I wait for Yve to get ready and then head downstairs for breakfast with her. Luca was still in bed when I got up and so I let him sleep. By the emptiness of the old restaurant, it looks as though a lot of people are making the most of a lie-in, but I'm still too wired to sleep in. Ham's sitting alone at a table eating, and so Yve and I join him. Despite having been in the army before the GDO came to power, and most of his old unit being here, Ham feels like one of us. He joined the army when he was eighteen, two years before the GDO were formed, and so he's still in his mid-twenties, unlike most of his unit. He was brought in to their unit as a sniper, because theirs had been killed. It must be hard to have to take over from someone in those circumstances. Maybe that's why he enjoys spending time with our group of misfits.

"How's the kid?" he asks Yve.

"A wriggly little bugger." Yve sips her coffee. "This coffee tastes like piss." She grimaces.

"Carl's having to ration it."

"What I wouldn't give for a proper cup of coffee — not one of those fancy whipped cream, cinnamon infused, handpicked and polished nonsense that we used to get. Just good old filter coffee, black and so strong it dissolves the inside of your stomach."

"Did you ever go to Danni's Diner?" I ask Yve.

"The one with the Danish pastries? They had the *best* coffee."

"And the pastries." We both sigh at the memory.

"Where you both from?" Ham asks us.

"Cass is from Auria, although aren't your parent's originally from Italy?" Yve asks me.

"Both my grandparents were, yeah," I reply.

"And I lived there for three years as a refugee with my mum, but I'm originally from Sweden."

"What about you?" I ask him.

"Aurian through and through, how else do you think I got into the army?"

"Did *you* ever eat at Danni's?"

"Sadly, I missed out, I was too busy drinking fancy hand-polished coffees," he smirks.

"And you call yourself an Aurian? Heathen," Yve scolds.

"Hey, did you get a letter from your mum the other day?" I ask Yve.

"Yeah, she wants to turn Vayo into a commune." Yve rolls her eyes and smiles fondly.

"What about your family?" I ask Ham, and I'm nervous asking because in times like these, not many people have their families.

"My three brothers are also in the Resistance but we've all ended up in different units. My parents are helping out the Resistance in Auria — we're a family of rebels." He shrugs but I can tell he's proud.

"Talk to me about these three brothers of yours." Yve leans forward.

"Well, I'm the handsomest."

"Obviously," she replies.

"And the youngest and the only one who is single." He leans in closer to her, a charming smile on his face, his eyes alight with humour.

"Fascinating, I wonder why that is? Poor hygiene?" She practically purrs.

Ham rallies despite the rebuff. "You'd be surprised how few female soldiers we've had until recently."

"Ah, I see." Yve nods sagely and then gets up. "Anyone want more pee-tasting coffee?" We shake our heads as she goes to the coffee urn.

Ham watches her walk away and I take the opportunity to gently remind him about Jake, but he says that he knows and gives me a kind smile, one that says whatever happens, he'll take care of my best friend. I decide it's time for me to leave so I get up and grab some food for Luca and Rage and head upstairs.

I leave Luca's food by the bed and then go in to see Rage. She's awake and dressed when I walk into Yve's room. I hold out the sandwich I made her, which she thanks me for, and then sits down on the end of the bed and wolfs it down.

"It's going to be a long day planning this operation."

"I know. I'm ready for this. I've been ready for this for years." And I know she means it but I can't help worrying what all this planning will bring up for her, especially considering her recent loss.

I make my way downstairs with Rage, and she goes to join Carl in the kitchen whilst I join Luca and the others, who clearly don't think Ham and Yve need some alone time. There's still a strange tension in the air. All of us have been shaken by the events of the day before.

Luca pulls me onto his lap and gives me a big, loud kiss, which makes everyone else groan.

"You two are disgusting," Jono gripes.

"Revolting," Drummer concurs.

"You should be separated," Yve agrees.

"You come in here and ruin our breakfast," Jono whines, and so Luca steals some of his bread, which makes him whine some more.

"How's your leg?" I ask him, and he continues to complain about hardly being able to sleep. Drummer then hands him his painkillers.

"Can you just take your meds now so we don't have to put up with your moaning all day?"

"I can't have them on an empty stomach! The doctor said!"

"You are such a baby when you're ill or in pain," Drummer sighs, and shakes two pills out of the bottle he's holding and watches Jono as he swallows them. "Good boy." Drummer pats him on the head. None of us ask him how Pranav is doing, although we're all concerned. But when he gets up to leave we all know that he's going to him and so we fall silent, to which Drummer nods, acknowledging our sentiment.

Later, we're all seated in the old conference room. Dune has decided to keep half of the Resistance fighters at the hotel, working on the Paris attack and coordinating with other units, whilst the other half focus on the raid of the GDO compound that holds the children. All of Sault, even Jono despite his injury, has insisted on being involved in the mission — Rage is one of us now, and we will fight on her behalf, always.

Dune has found the old screen the hotel would use for meetings and has managed to connect his tablet to it. On the screen is an aerial map of the area we intend to attack.

"Thanks to the intel we've been given from the Bernhem intelligence team and Rage, we have the exact location of the site, along with up-to-date aerial footage." He zooms in on a large building and two smaller ones.

"The complex is larger than we anticipated and, excluding the children, there are as far as we know fifty-two GDO personnel on site." I'm shocked by how many there are; I didn't think it was such a large base of operation. "Our best guess of the number of children at the complex is... two hundred and fifty." None of us expected that. My stomach sinks. It was bad enough knowing they had them, but so many? "It's a much bigger operation than we originally planned for, and we're going to work in conjunction with Bernhem as the base relies heavily on next-gen tech. They're also going to be sending in support vehicles to transport the children."

"Where will the children go?" I ask.

"Back to Auria, it's the only place that's safe enough to send them. The Aurians are working on finding housing for them and they'll try and reconnect them with their families, if they can."

Dune continues to talk us through the setup at the site and asks Rage the odd question. We have to plan this operation meticulously; we know we'll only get one shot at it. We can't pull more forces into the mission because they are currently targeting the GDO's air force bases to prevent any further air raids, and then they'll be focusing on Paris. We're all

that those two hundred and fifty children have, and
I don't think we're enough.

RAGE

As Rage listens to the plans that Dune is slowly pulling together, she feels an odd sense of dread. This isn't going to work. None of their plans so far has. There is no way that their team of thirty-five can take on a base that large, and they seem to be forgetting that most of the children housed there are already well trained enough to fight back. Before Knight had been murdered, she would talk with him about the base and how they would destroy it. Knight said he'd put provisions in place to ensure that the young recruits would fight against the GDO, and he'd begun to lay the groundwork. They just needed a code phrase, he said, something that would trigger the internal rebellion. They'd made plans, they'd laid it all out, but now that he was gone, they would never be enacted.

When the meeting is over, Rage decides to go for a walk. Knight's dream of saving all those kids is over. There is no way they can achieve it now. She is going to fail him. Her head begins to fill with the blackness and her ears begin to ring. Her heart beats faster and faster. Is this how she is going to die? Taunted by her imaginary demons? She leans on a nearby tree, trying to control her breathing, and then senses someone approaching. She spins around, her eyes slightly unfocused, a knife in her hand. It's Luca. She puts her knife away and turns away from him.

Luca sits down on the ground and doesn't say anything, which is why she likes him. When she first met him, she thought he was boring, but really, he's just quiet, considered. She can see why Cassia loves him, this silent force, ready to protect those he loves with everything he has.

"I've failed him."

"No you haven't."

"It's not going to work."

"We've only just started planning — we'll make it work." She turns back to face him, her haunted eyes stormy.

"We'll fail and all those other kids will suffer. They will be punished and you can't even imagine what that kind of punishment is like."

"Which is why we're not going to fail. I won't let them take anything else from you, none of us will."

"You can't make promises like that, you just can't." She's frustrated with him now.

"Rae, we won't fail. We will cover every scenario, plan for every outcome. We will be thorough. We will be careful. We won't let you down."

"You don't know that!" Rage punches Luca's arm in frustration.

"Yes I do."

"No you don't, no you don't, no you don't," she repeats as she punches him until he holds her tiny fists in his massive hands.

"Yes I do." Rage breaks down then and Luca holds her as the sunlight begins to fade in the woods. The leaves are golden in the late light, and a few fall and join the blanket of leaves that covers the ground. All is silent except for the sobs of an orphaned child who the world was cruel to, who has lost hope. But she is sheltered in the arms of her protector and he will fight for her, and so will his team.

CASSIA

I watch as Luca follows Rage, and I give them some time before I go to join them. It's getting dark and cold when I finally see them. Rage is curled up in his arms. He looks up at me, desperate, and I know what he's feeling. He wants to take her pain away, to fix it all for her. It's how I feel but we cannot bring Night back. We can only try to put an end to the horrors that the GDO are committing in the compound. Rage turns when she sees me and stands up.

"We're going to get them out?" she asks, uncertain.

"Absolutely." I hide my doubts and let her believe we can do this. We begin to walk back. "Do you know what I think you need?" She doesn't respond. "To beat the crap out of something." She looks up at me, interested. I lead her through the hotel to a back room that would have once been used for meetings but we've cleared out all the tables and chairs. Jono is sitting against the wall with Pranav, whom I'm happy to see has left his room. Ham, Ellyas, Drummer, and Yve are waiting for us.

"Finally!" Drummer beams at us. I go and sit with Pranav and Jono, my arm still too weak for me to participate.

"Right, squirt, you're looking out of shape so we decided on a training session. I mean, look at these arms." Ham wraps his hand easily around her upper arm. "Pitiful."

"I bet I could beat all of you," Rage says with her old bravado.

"Oh hooooo, a challenge!" Ham punches her lightly in the arm.

"All at once?" Yve asks.

Rage considers it. "One at a time. I'm out of practice." The others manage to hold in their smiles. "Who's up first? And none of this letting me win because I'm small."

"Wouldn't dream of it," Ham exclaims as he squares up to her. The others step back to watch.

Ham lunges for Rage and she karate chops him in the throat. He stops in his tracks instantly and lets out a stream of curse words.

"Hey, you didn't say a clean fight." A smile tugs at her lips. I suppose I should be concerned that violence is what's cheering her up, but I decide not to think about it too much and instead worry about where she's going to hit Luca.

"Wait, one rule!" Drummer says in a panic. "No punching our balls."

"Or boobs," adds Yve.

"Ugh, fine, you bunch of wimps." Rage crosses her arms. "Who's next?" Luca steps forward, reluctantly. Rage trips him before he even has a chance to do anything. "Next!" she yells as Luca rubs his head in pain and confusion. Ellyas laughs loudly at seeing his brother beaten by a child.

"The kid fights dirty," Yve laments, but I know Yve and she fights dirty, too. Before Yve even announces that she's next, she rugby tackles Rage by diving for her legs, grabbing them so that Rage collapses on top of her. Yve then flips Rage over and sits on her. "Honestly boys, I can't believe you let someone so small beat you. OW!" Yve yelps as Rage bites her. "Right, that's it. Ham, lift this wretch." Ham happily complies by lifting Rage up over his shoulder. "It's time you learned some manners, Miss Rage." Yve storms down the hall towards the kitchen with Ham in tow, Rage over his shoulder, and the rest of us following, wondering what exactly Yve's plan is. She leads us through the kitchen to the back pantry where an old chest freezer is humming away. She lifts the lid and Ham dutifully complies by plonking Rage inside. She lets out a scream, and Yve and Ham stop her from climbing out but don't shut the lid on her.

"Do you surrender?" Yve demands.

"Never," Rage huffs as she tries to push Ham out of the way.

"Surrender or suffer the consequences."

"*Never.*"

"Drummer, pass the suspicious-looking container," Yve orders. Drummer picks up a huge tub of greenish-looking sludge, something we've avoided since we arrived and we suspect is probably rancid mayonnaise.

Drummer starts to unscrew the lid and we all gag at the smell. "No... wait!" Rage clambers to the back of the freezer. "I surrender."

"Please screw the lid back on," Jono begs as we all cover our mouths and noses. Drummer does so — as the closest, he's struggling the most with the stench.

"Hey! What you doing trampling all over our food, shrimp?" Carl yells from the doorway. "And what the hell is that smell?!"

We all look to Rage and she rolls her eyes. "That was me." And with that, we call a truce and let her out of the freezer. Drummer declares this makes up for her never having had a proper initiation, which reminds us that Ham hasn't either, but none of us is entirely sure how to get him into the freezer and so we leave it alone.

WEEK THIRTY-THREE

CASSIA

The planning process is going slowly. With our numbers being so low and theirs so high, we have to be meticulous and we have to think of every single possible angle. Rage has become restless, training daily at our makeshift firing range, inventing more and more elaborate assault courses with Ham, which, I have to admit, are pretty fun even though they're ridiculously gruelling, particularly with a bad shoulder. Some nights she shares a room with Yve, others she sleeps on the floor in my and Luca's room, mostly because she gets fed up with Yve for some petty reason. Despite all that she's lost, she's holding up well.

Pranav is quieter than before, which is unsurprising, and Drummer spends most of his time alone with him, which has left Jono a little more aimless than usual, and seeing as his leg won't heal for a while, he's getting restless, and a restless Jono is a dangerous affair. He's begun pulling pranks and always manages to do them at unfortunate times, like booby trapping a door with water and flour and Dune being the first one to walk through it. They're the sort of pranks you pulled when you were twelve, the sort that Rage thinks are hilarious and so has decided to help him out, which has had her banished from our room for an entire night after an unfortunate cling-filmed toilet incident that Luca was subjected to. I found it pretty funny until he threatened for me to clean it up.

Christmas comes, and it feels like it's out of nowhere. We celebrate together, and Hippo vs Lion is reprised, along with a few other invented games. We laugh. We pretend. We even manage to find the hotel's old decorations to hang. But as the morning of the twenty-sixth dawns, we are back to being soldiers again.

Now that two weeks have passed, we're all anxious to get on with the plan. It doesn't feel right staying in one place when a war is going on, whilst the others in the hotel are going out on missions almost daily. Although, it has been nice to finally feel like I'm in a regular relationship with Luca — doing activities together (granted, violent ones) and sharing a room at night. It feels normal and really, really good. The bubble we've created has been keeping out my thoughts of Kohler; I can pretend here in this abandoned, rundown hotel that Kohler doesn't exist, even if he does still slip into my nightmares like a lingering shadow.

Finally, though, Dune decides that we're as prepared as we'll ever be and it's time to set our plan in motion. Despite his injury, Jono has insisted on joining us and liaising directly with Bernhem from our temporary camp, kind of like a base of operations. The journey is uneventful and the setup of our camp is straightforward. Jono repeatedly makes jokes about our military precision, which was only funny the first three times.

Dune decides to put Yve and me in a tent with Rage, which is fine but I'll miss sharing with Luca. And of course, none of us can sleep when we turn in. Rage is particularly hyper.

"Did they give you coffee again?" Yve asks from under her sleeping bag where she's trying to hide from Rage's incessant chattering.

"No, just have a lot of energy."

"Would it be wrong to drug her?" I enquire, with sincerity.

"Depends on what you plan on using."

"Oooo, can I try the stuff they gave Jono in hospital when he went all loopy?"

"No," Yve and I say in unison.

"It sounded really fun," she whines.

"When did we start parenting a brat?" Yve speculates out loud.

"The day we tweezed shrapnel out of her ass," I respond.

"You guys are no fun. I wish I was sharing with the boys."

"No you don't, they fart so much," Yve reveals to her.

"Yeah... 'spose."

"Rae, can't you count sheep or something, we really need to get as much sleep as possible," I say as gently as I can.

"Maybe I'll just join Ellyas and Luca on first watch."

"Fine, but you need to come back after and get some sleep. I don't want you shooting your own foot off, or mine for that matter, because you're shattered," I scold.

"Yeah, yeah," she sighs as she unzips her sleeping bag. "You're *such* a mum."

She leaves the tent and I turn to Yve. "I'm not a mum, am I?"

"Oh, sweetie, lie to yourself all you like."

I attempt a retort but give up, turn onto my back, and look up at the canvas tent above. I can hear the soft voices of the rest of our camp — the snap of twigs, the click of a gun being cleaned. These are the sounds that lull me to sleep, sounds of ammunition and soldiers. I wonder, as I drift off, if after all this I'll be able to sleep without them.

RAGE

Rage keeps telling herself she'll go to sleep after the next shift change, but every time one comes around she still feels too jittery to even contemplate rest, let alone sleep. The company she keeps is quiet; being on watch, there can't be too much interaction — they're too close to the compound to take such a risk. And maybe that's why she can't sleep, she reasons, because she's close to where Knight was brutally murdered. She knows it was brutal. She heard it.

She shakes the thought, the screams, from her head. Instead, she walks the perimeter, her rifle always ready, ever the diligent soldier; it's all she's ever known. She hears movement nearby and raises her weapon and waits, still and silent. Jono emerges from the darkness, buckling up his belt.

"Jeez, I nearly shot you."

"No you didn't." Jono smiles at her.

"I did, I'm so tired my trigger finger is starting to spasm."

"Well, in that case, you need to sleep."

"Can't."

"Tents, they do that and give you backache."

"Yeah, and Yve and Cassia nag me."

"They *nag* you? Oh, that won't do." Jono puts his hands on his hips.

"No, no pranks. Not tonight."

"Who are you and what have you done with my partner in crime?"

Rage looks around and shrugs, not wanting to have to say no to Jono, but she doesn't have the energy for pranks or shenanigans. Tonight she is too focused on the mission ahead.

"You know what? I kinda feel like sitting down for a bit, I'm too tired to mess with people." He leans on his right leg, taking the weight off his injured one.

"Yeah, me too." She gives him a half smile and he gives her a friendly elbow.

"And maybe when our shift ends we trap Luca, Ellyas, and Ham inside their tent?"

"Okay, that does sound a little fun."

Rage is finally asleep when everyone begins packing up their gear, but they let her sleep, allowing her the luxury of not having to load up vehicles and check inventory. Cassia eventually wakes her and Rage instinctively punches her in response, which Cassia doesn't take too well.

"We have a briefing." Cassia rubs her cheek and glares at Rage.

"Mmmmfph."

Cassia pulls Rage's sleeping bag off her, and Rage curls into a ball.

"I will loose Jono and Drummer on you." Rage punches Cassia again.

CASSIA

I can't believe I'm about to raid a GDO facility with a black eye thanks to a twelve-, maybe thirteen-year-old who can land a punch in her sleep. I'd throw water over her as payback but sadly we don't have an ice-cold bucketful handy. Instead I join the others and triple-check my gear; I don't think I've ever been this thorough before. I don't think the odds have ever been so heavily against us — we failed Troyes and here we are trying to rescue vulnerable and dangerous children. Despite the odds, I know that when the reward is great, it's worth putting it all on the line. Rage joins us and the final recap commences. We sit in concentrated silence. Every detail matters; we will give this our all.

"I feel like most of our time has been spent travelling to destinations," Drummer says quietly through the head mic that's attached to his radio.

"At least this time we don't have to worry about Jono's pre-battle voms," Luca responds.

"Just because I'm not with you doesn't mean I can't hear you," Jono says from his support station back at base camp. He's not alone. Just before we left Clive showed up with a couple of other intelligence agents and his mum. Apparently, they all wanted to get more involved with missions.

Honestly, none of us minded, because Linda brought homemade brownies and it was nice to see Clive again. I'd also asked him to do something for me and he'd come through, as always. He handed me a small package and I gave him a tight hug as thanks. We were also happy to have Clive there as I don't think any of us were particularly confident in having Jono running our intelligence ops.

"This is why we need helicopters," Rage says, "so that we can just parachute in everywhere instead of walking for *miles* or driving for *miles*."

"Shame there aren't any at the compound we can steal," I reply, my voice barely audible but clear on the radio. We're all handling our nerves better today, although Luca and I keep catching each other's eyes and accidentally gravitating towards one another. I guess it's an unconscious security thing.

The building has now come into view. In plain sight, it looks like a large u-shaped office complex. Dune halts us and nods to Pranav who sets down a remote-control drone rigged with a camera and a few small packages courtesy of Rage.

We watch and wait as he flies the drone straight for the base, high enough and quiet enough that it may not be detected. We're anticipating it'll be seen, but we might get lucky. So far, no one's shouted or tried to shoot it down, which is exactly what we want.

Dune monitors the screen that displays the drone's video feed as Pranav flies the drone towards the back of the compound and releases one of the packages. The bomb explodes on impact taking out the generator. We watch the ensuing panic and the soldiers spilling out from inside the building, but we don't move.

"Okay, are you both ready?" Dune asks as Rage and I step forward.

"Ready," I say, giving Luca's hand a final squeeze, whilst Ellyas rests his hand on his brother's shoulder, keeping him strong. Rage leads the way down a slight incline towards an underpass. As we reach it, another bomb is dropped, this time on the main gate. We walk through the tunnel beneath the main road, and instead of blowing open the lock on the door that is concealed in the passageway, we use a new device that Bernhem sent us. I hold it up to the keypad and wait until the light on the electronic lock turns green. We pass through the doorway and up some steps into the compound. We hear soldiers open fire on the drone as we run and approach a smaller building that is set slightly apart from the main one — Rage had explained it's where the GDO took you when you were being "disciplined". With the sound of gunfire now all around, the others having opened fire on the GDO camp, I unlock the door using the same gadget. I pull on the handle and it reluctantly gives. We slip inside, and Rage pushes open a door that leads to another tunnel she'd discovered in one of her escape attempts. It will lead us straight to the main building, straight to our enemy.

Rage turns to me. "Hold my hand whilst I take you down the darkest paths," she says, and I know she means metaphorically as well as literally. Rage will lead me to where her burning hatred glows, and I will happily tumble into it and forget who I was and what I believed so that I might turn my pain to ash and my misery to vapour. I put my hand into her small one, and I don't wonder who she could have been anymore. This is who she is. She is the embodiment of revenge and so I follow her — not the child others see, but the wrathful, avenging angel come for retribution.

We emerge at another door and we can hear people running down the hallway on the other side. We wait for Dune's signal. "Release," he announces over our radios, and we open the door into a chaotic hallway where only dim emergency lighting reveals our position. Two soldiers turn to us when the grenades thrown by the Resistance outside explode one by one; the distraction is all we need to take out the two soldiers. We leave them unconscious as we turn to face the other three in the hall. They raise their guns, and I'm relieved they aren't children as I throw an ES grenade, a little something one of our raiding parties found. They fall and we jump over them, Rage leading the way. She stops outside a door and I stand beside her, my back against the wall. She glances into the room, assessing the situation lightning quick. I pull out my grenade, but she shakes her head once. This is hers. She flicks the pin out with her thumb and I kick open the door as she throws the grenade inside. I pull her away from the doorway as the room erupts in an explosion of flames and screams, destroying their operation centre — a place where none of the young recruits are allowed to work for fear of what they might learn and then share amongst themselves.

"Go," I say into my radio; with the operation centre down, our team can advance. Rage leads the way and the white hall curves to the left and opens out onto a set of lifts. There's a door on the right, which Rage opens, and we make our way down the stairs to the basement. There's only one room down here and it's badly lit and smells musty. It's filled with banks of desks with computers where children are sitting, working. Children, dozens of them.

I'd asked Rage how to gain their trust, but she told me I couldn't and that they'd kill me on the spot. "Knight was going to imbed a trigger code into the GDO programming."

"And did he?"

"He didn't have the chance." But I had never believed that — from what Rage told me, Night was the one who was more willing to risk it all to fight the GDO.

Almost as one they rise and grab their weapons, which are strapped beneath the tables in front of them, and aim them at us. Rage has frozen to the spot, not prepared to see this stark reminder of her life before.

I take a leap of faith and in a clear, calm voice I say, "The mountains are coming down." A flicker of emotion crosses a few of the steely faces before me.

The youngest, a girl with knotted blonde hair, dark-rimmed eyes, and cracked lips whispers, "Rage Rage Rage." The other children look around, unsure of what to do, and I turn to Rage. Her face is blank, remembering her loss.

I hold her face in my hands. "Rae... Rae, look at me." She raises her eyes to mine. "You need to lead them out, you are the one who needs to do this. They trust you, okay?" She blinks and then nods slowly.

"Rage will get you all to safety." I turn back to her and kiss her on top of her head and I feel a heaviness inside, one weighted with foreboding. There are more children to save and I have one person in particular I need to face.

KOHLER

When the first bomb went off, Major Kohler was in the war room. He told everyone to stay put and remain calm, but he had no control over people outside of the room he was commanding. He sent a base-wide 'com, but those outside didn't listen. They went outside to face the attackers, which was clearly part of the Resistance plan to lure them outside. How they'd won the war with idiots like these he'd never understand.

He watched the feeds from outside the perimeter. He could feel her; he knew she was near. Then he saw her approach with that treacherous little girl. He ordered the room to lock in the recruits and stormed out towards his office. When he was there collecting his sidearm, he heard the explosion come from inside the base. *Clever little Fortis*, he thought as he moved. He caught up with her as she emerged from the basement — the last to leave after having ushered the children out. But he didn't give a damn about the brats — no, she was what he wanted.

Her hair was tied in its usual high ponytail; little wisps had escaped around the front, framing her face with a halo of tiny curls. He took in her almond eyes, her mouth now set in a grim line, her dimpled chin, and he thought how much he'd love to smash his fist into it. The thought aroused him.

"There was no need for such a dramatic entrance; I would have welcomed you here."

She didn't go for small talk; instead, she stepped forward and threw a punch. Kohler hadn't expected it at all, and she caught him on the lip, splitting it. A shudder of satisfaction ran through him.

"I'm going to really enjoy this," Kohler said as he grabbed her by the ponytail and pulled it down.

"Like your dad did?" The remark made him falter and he loosened his grip enough for Cassia to kick him in the shin and then elbow him in the kidney. "Did you forget that I wasn't the only one who let things slip through the cracks? How is the general? Keeping an eye on you as usual?"

Kohler slapped her hard across the face; the impact threw her backwards and she hit her head against the wall. He flattened himself against her and whispered in her ear, "Remember this?"

"Remember this?!" Cassia retorted and triggered her ES gun from her pocket right into his groin. The shock ran through him into her but she didn't care; it was worth it to hear his screams. She kicked him off her and he stumbled back. "It's a shame I couldn't reach my other gun," she said as she stepped forward.

"You little bitch."

"Ugh, really? That's the best you can do?" Cassia threw a punch, which Kohler blocked. He grabbed her wrist and she twisted and side kicked him in the leg. He then wrapped his arm around her neck and started to choke her; she could feel against her thigh how much he was enjoying it. She tries to kick but doesn't make contact. She's beginning to struggle to breathe as he pants with ecstasy at her panic.

"I will always be in your head."

"No you won't." Cassia lashes her head backwards and into his nose; he loosens his grip and she twists free. Kohler fumbles for his gun, but Cassia pulls hers at the same time.

"Looks like we have a stand-off." He smirks at her, blood dripping from his nose into his mouth."

"No we don't." She fires at the same time he does.

RAGE

Rage manages to get the children from the basement out through the tunnel and the underpass. She leads them away from the compound as the Resistance act as a distraction, drawing the GDO's focus away from them. She leads them to a secluded spot where the people from Bernhem are waiting with vehicles to transport the kids out of there. They're all dazed and uncertain when they reach the buses, none of them trusting the people holding guns, and it takes all of Rage's patience and persuasive skills to convince them to get on board.

As soon as Rage feels she can, she leaves and heads back to the compound. She radios Cassia but doesn't get a response; she begins to feel alarmed and starts to run. There's a soldier in the outer building when she arrives, so she shoots him and he falls back winded, his bullet-proof vest having stopped the bullet. She kicks him in the head for good measure and then enters the tunnel. Inside the main building, she finds ten GDO soldiers either tied up or dead, which means some of the Resistance have managed to get inside. She runs down the hall and turns when she hears approaching footsteps. It's Luca and Yve. Rage lowers her rifle.

"Where's Cass?" Luca asks, his panic evident.

Rage can't reply; instead, she turns and begins to run down the corridor towards the door that leads to the basement, the last place she saw her. She stops dead when she reaches the lifts — Cassia's lying on the floor and so is a GDO soldier.

"No!" Luca gasps and goes to her. He bends over her body and she opens her eyes.

"Ow," she breathes as Luca frantically checks her body until he finds the bullet hole in her chest and the bullet lodged in her bullet-proof vest. Luca lets out a choking laugh-sob.

"I thought..."

"I'd been shot? Well, it feels like I have." Cassia takes a slow deep breath.

"This dude is still breathing," Yve says as she nudges Kohler's body.

"Well, that's a shame," Cassia says as she slowly sits up.

"A real shame." Luca's voice is low and menacing. Rage takes a closer look at the man who is slowly coming around. His ice blue eyes and light blond hair are familiar — the same eyes as the general.

"Kohler?" Rage says as she sees his name stitched into his uniform. So he is definitely related to the general. "Where's your dad?"

"He left two days ago."

"Shame, I have some things I want to say to him." Rage strokes her gun lovingly as she says this.

"We need to get moving," Cassia says as Luca helps her to her feet. She's taking in long slow breaths, clearly badly winded from the bullet.

"What about this turd?" Yve asks as she kicks him.

"I know a place," Rage says with a wicked smile.

Rage and Yve help Kohler to his feet and then drag him through the tunnel to the outbuilding whilst Luca and Cassia re-join the efforts to free the children, whom the GDO have now barricaded inside one building, afraid that they'll join the fight against them instead of for them. They hadn't anticipated a scenario like this, and there was no telling how the recruits would react.

Rage removes the prison keys from the enraged soldier who is still tied to the radiator where she'd left him not long before. She takes a deep breath before opening the door, not knowing if there would be anyone inside. Dune announces on the radio that they've breached the building that held the children and they have joined them in the fight, and that anyone in the other buildings should begin checking for survivors. Rage pauses at the door and messages Cassia.

"There are fifteen cells here. You and Luca might want to give us a hand." She turns to look at Yve — strong, proud Yve who will not be prepared for what's behind the doors. "Just be gentle with them." Yve's hand rests on Rage's shoulder, and it's only then that she realises she's shaking. She opens the first door. The sour smell hits her first; she turns on the light to the dark cell, which only has the smallest of windows. In the corner of the solitary bed, dirty and bruised, is a girl about Rage's age. She tightens her arms around her knees and then, when her eyes have adjusted, she stares at Rage with disbelief.

"Saviour?" she asks, her voice hoarse.

"No, I'm Rage, and this is Yve. We've come to get you out."

"Saviour." The girl slowly stands on unsteady legs and then steps forward and hugs Rage. "Saviour." Rage doesn't say anything back; instead, she leads the girl out and sits her down in the guards' break room. Yve then leads a withstrained Kohler past them both, and the girl spits at him. Yve locks him in the cell and Rage goes through the cupboards and pulls out packets of biscuits and bottles of water. She hands them to the girl.

"Do you think you can be in charge of handing these out to everyone?"

She gives Rage a wonky smile and then bites into a biscuit hungrily. Luca and Cassia walk in just as Rage and Yve are about to start opening up more cells. When Cassia sees the girl, Rage can tell it takes everything for Cassia to keep her emotions under control. Cassia walks over to the girl and introduces herself.

"Do you think it would be okay if I had a biscuit?" The girl holds out the packet for her. "Thank you, that's very kind of you. What's your name?"

"I'm not allowed a name yet."

"Of course you are. What was your name before? Maybe we can call you that?"

The girl thinks for a moment and then whispers, "Sophie."

"That's a very pretty name." Cassia stands. "I'm just going to help the others now, Sophie." She turns to see Luca watching her and wearing an expression that speaks of love and pride. Rage's arms are crossed over her body and she can tell Yve is trying her best to focus on anything else, trying not to let herself get emotional.

"Okay," Cassia says to them and steps forward. Rage holds out the key to her, not willing to do it alone. Cassia takes a breath and slides the key into the lock.

CASSIA

I turn the lock in the plain grey door and slowly push it open. It is the ninth door I've opened; three of the previous rooms were empty, and in one, a little boy wasn't breathing, his tiny frame stiff and cool to touch. We'd pulled a blanket over him and we'll bury him properly before we go. My heart feels splintered and heavy as the door creaks on its hinges. There's a little boy wearing white shorts and a white t-shirt sitting on the side of his bed, metal-framed with a thin mattress; I try not to think of the other little boy who didn't make it. He looks up at me with big, brown eyes, his dark hair curling around his ears. His arm is in a brace, the cuts covering his legs and arms are scabbed, his injuries old. His eyes are pools of pain, of unspeakable injustice, and it takes all my strength not to show how the sight of him makes me feel. I step forward slowly and sit down next to him.

"My name is Cassia, I'm here with my friends to get you out of here." His eyes speak to me. Some sort of recognition shows in them, but I don't know what they're saying. I hold out my hand to him and he slips his small hand into mine. "We have biscuits and warm clothes," I say to him as I lead him out of the room towards the break room where Yve and

Luca are handing out clothes they'd found in a storage cupboard. Rage shuts the door next to the room I've come out of and turns to me, then freezes. The little boy lets go of my hand and runs to her, buries his face in her chest. Her arms go round him instinctively.

"Knight?" Her voice trembles and she squeezes him tighter. "Knight!" We're all frozen watching the reunion, wondering how on earth it could be possible for Night to be alive.

Dune's voice in my radio snaps me out of my trance. "Status on hostages?"

"Five more cells to go, one deceased," Yve reports.

"Things turned quickly here thanks to the children siding with us. They kept chanting something about mountains coming down. Any idea what that's about?"

"Yeah, I think I do," I say as I watch Rage and Night.

"We're moving to the drop-off now. We'll see you up there." He signs off.

"Rae, why don't you get Night something to eat and drink?" I say gently, trying to bring her out of her shock. She looks up at me and smiles in a way I've never seen her smile before; it pierces my heart with the purity of it. I unlock the next five doors. Four of the rooms are occupied, and each of the children is in a bad way, malnourished, covered in cuts and bruises, shivering with cold. We make sure that all of them have enough clothes on, and Luca manages to find the locker with their shoes in. Night is one of the weakest, and so with Rage's permission, which she gives with strict instructions for him to be super careful, Luca carries him. The youngest girl, who can't be more than seven, is very frail and so I carry her and Yve takes the hands of a boy and girl who are a little unsteady. We step out into the freezing afternoon and make our way towards the others. The little girl in my arms wraps her arms around my neck.

"Is it safe?" she asks me.

"Yes, it's safe."

When we reach the buses Dune is coordinating everyone. The children we have are the ones in the worst condition, and so they are led to another bus where they can be checked over by a doctor. There's a change in the atmosphere — it doesn't feel like a victory, not when these children have been through so much. I try to pass the little girl in my arms to another soldier but she won't let me go, and so I take her onto the bus and sit her down.

"It's safe here, you're safe here." She looks up at me and her bottom lip begins to wobble, but I tear myself away — I have something I need to do.

I step down from the bus and stand staring at what's around us. All these lost souls, so young, so innocent. Stolen from their childhoods, abused, shattered. Luca approaches me and I want to speak but the words feel lodged in my throat. I look up at him, tall, imposing, but yet so kind and gentle.

I hesitate but eventually manage to say, "I… I want to go with them." I hadn't really realised this is what I wanted until I spoke the words, and they feel right, more right than anything I've done in the last few weeks.

His eyes are sad as he says, "I know."

"You do? I didn't know until just now," I say with confusion.

"I think I saw it the first time you realised there were children who needed us."

"Luca, I…"

He pulls me into a hug. "It's okay."

I begin to cry. "But I can't leave you."

"Yes you can."

"I don't want to leave you."

"I know, but this is what you want." I can feel his heart beating faster than normal, telling me of his pain.

"I hate that you're so understanding." He looks down at me and I think I can see tears in his eyes.

"Not this time, but you haven't wanted to fight this war for a long time. You have another one that needs fighting. I'm not going to ask you to stay." I pull him closer, breathe him in. Am I really going to do this? Just like that?

"But we're not on a break or breaking up or anything," he says, firmly.

"Absolutely not." I squeeze even harder.

"I'm just sorry that our paths aren't the same right now."

"But they will be again." I stand on my tiptoes as I kiss him. "I love you always."

"I love you always," he says back, and I don't think I can do this, walk away from him and the cause I risked everything for, but then I see Night walking hand-in-hand with Rage and I know I don't really have a choice. These children deserve better and I want to help give them that. Maybe with some time away to help them heal, I can somehow heal myself and I can come back to Luca, to the war.

After speaking with Dune, I walk over to where Ellyas and Yve are patching up each other's wounds; Jono is nearby so I signal him over. When Drummer sees us gathering, he brings Pranav with him. I can feel Rage nearby but she doesn't approach.

"I'm going to help get the children to Vayo and then assist in their recovery." I catch Rage's change in expression; she's shut me out already.

Yve looks like she wants to punch me, which she might. "You're really doing this? Leaving... just like that?"

"I'm really doing this." She turns away from me and my heart clenches.

"But before I go, I asked Clive to make something for us. For Sault squad." I pull out the package that's been stashed in my combat trousers pocket. I open it and hand them each a small fabric disk. On it is a lion, similar to the one my dad has on his medallion, and the same slogan encircles it, "Quidvis recte factum quamvis humile praeclarum". Whatever is rightly done, however humble, is noble. Above the lion's head it says 'sault' and below 'squad'. There's also one for Ham and Dune, I give them to Luca to hand out.

Drummer looks down at the patch in his hand, running his finger over the stitching, "Pranav and I were thinking the same thing." Drummer says, and Jono looks like he's actually been punched in the gut by Yve.

"Anyone else feel like deserting?" Jono crosses his arms and glares at us all. I swallow hard as a lump in my throat forms. I feel like a traitor.

Drummer turns to Luca. "We'll watch out for her."

"I know you will." His smile is pained and I cup his cheek with my hand, wanting to stay but needing to leave. I turn to Rage who is glaring at me.

"Rae, I'm going to look out for all these kids, I'm not abandoning you." She's refusing to look at me. Night nudges her.

"Knight wants to know if he can stay with you."

"Of course he can."

"His parents are dead so he's got nobody but me. You gotta look after him, okay?"

"I promise."

"And see if someone can fix his Symbio link — Kohler smashed it, that's why I thought he was dead." She scuffs her foot along the floor. "'Cos we are going to have to have our 'coms removed."

"I know some great doctors."

"Because he can't stay and fight." She looks at me then, her eyes filling with tears. "It isn't safe for him." Fat tears fall down Night's face as she talks, and she turns to face him. "And I'm gonna come back for you, when I've fixed everything." She squeezes him tight, and when she lets go she pulls me aside.

"There's something you need to know…" She bites her bottom lip. "It's Knight, with a 'K', just… just so you get it right."

"Oh, I see. I'll make sure people know." I hesitate before asking, "Did you name him?"

"Yeah, because…"

"It's okay, I get it." I pull her into a hug, which she tries and fails to resist. "I'm going to miss you."

"Don't worry, we'll fix this mess and come back in a few weeks." I try to look positive but I know how wars work. This won't be over in a few weeks, or even a few months. It could be years before this ends, one way or the other.

As I'm walking towards the bus, Yve grabs me and pulls me into an uncomfortably tight hug. "I'll never forgive you for this."

"I know, I'm sorry."

"Never be sorry for being you. I get it, I just don't want to."

"Look after the kid." She nods, biting her bottom lip hard, holding in whatever emotion she's refusing to betray.

Knight gets onto the bus and I go to Luca for a final goodbye. "I'll try and visit," he says.

"Me too," I say through tears that I haven't been able to hold back.

"It's not forever." And even though I know he's trying to be positive, we know it might be. Things in Auria could collapse, the journey back could be dangerous, but the worst part is that Luca is going to continue to fight.

I may never see him again.

Our goodbye feels too brief, but I go take my place on the bus next to Knight who looks up at me shyly, and I think about my decision as I look around at the children whom we rescued from the cells. If I continue fighting, I will be instrumental in the deaths of more people and I cannot bear that weight. But if I walk away, if I help these children, then I will finally be fixing something that was destroyed. And although I've walked away from Luca, walked away from our war, I chose my own path.

RAGE

Rage doesn't like feeling abandoned — with Cassia and Knight now gone, she feels lost. She'll even miss Drummer and Pranav; they were part of the team, her family. She sits on the floor in the dirt and refuses to help the others as they set up inside the GDO base so that they can spend a few nights discovering what the compound has to offer, maybe even taking it over as their own command centre. On his way back from dropping off a box of equipment, Luca stops and sits down next to Rage and decides to break convention, pulling her into a side hug.

"You've still got us."

"It's not the same."

"No, it isn't." He pauses and Rage doesn't want to look at him and see any terrifying intense emotion, so she keeps her eyes fixed to the ground. "We'll have to make do, stay busy, distracted."

Rage lets out a long slow breath. "Can we prank Ham?"

"Well, if you want to do that, we'll need to bring the master on board." Luca calls Jono over and he limps towards them, a despondent look on his face. "I'm sure he'll come up with something spectacular." And Rage almost smiles.

KOHLER

Major Jay Kohler sat in his cell dabbing his bloody lip, nose stuffed with pieces of cloth he'd ripped from his uniform. The bullet wound that was just below his shoulder had been strapped up. He'd lost a lot of blood and was surprised when the Resistance had insisted on stopping the bleeding. He should have realised that they wanted him alive for a reason.

He was still angry at the way things had turned out and felt like crap. The door to his room opened and two men stood there — one tall, dark-haired and imposing, the other shorter, rounder, and bald. The door shut behind them. He recognised the tall one as the leader of the Resistance cell Fortis was a part of, and the short one was their assassin.

"I'm so glad that you and I can finally have a little chat," the tall man said. A familiar flicker of fear burned in Kohler's stomach.

And he realised that today was to be the day he died.

WEEK THIRTY-EIGHT

CASSIA

When we reached Vayo my parents were still there, ready to greet me, to fold me into their arms and never let me go. Almost all of Auria has been retaken by the Resistance — the last nation to fall and the first to regain its feet. The government officials have relocated to Camburg — where this all began — to start rebuilding whilst the final GDO pockets are removed from Amphora, the capital.

Since I've been back we have gathered the kids together in groups for activities every day; sometimes they help us build something, paint something, and other times we play football and, at Knight's insistence, Hippos vs Lions. We've already managed to locate the families of fourteen of the children and found temporary homes for the majority of the rest. Knight is staying with me, and Emma has already taken him under her wing, enjoying having a brother again. I hate to think how Rae will react when she finds out.

I wake up early and go to meet Clive, Pranav, and Drummer — we are working on ways to destroy

GDO revenue streams remotely. It's strange to be working behind a computer again; it reminds me of my time working for the GDO. I log into my computer and check how the news of the Resistance is reaching citizens in Paris. We have the few people who are still connected to the internet working on our behalf, spreading the information that the Resistance is coming to free them. Our numbers are slowly growing. Soon, I believe, the tide will turn in our favour.

Before lunch I receive a video call from Luca. He's no longer at the farmhouse —Sault team, or what's left of it, has relocated. They're holed up in a small town, working to support the locals, increase Resistance support, and try to turn as many GDO soldiers as they can. He holds his tablet up and shows me Rage pinning Jono down for eating her last chocolate bar and Yve trying to prise her off. I miss them, I miss being part of the team, but my work here feels more important right now.

I eat my dinner with my parents, Emma, and Knight. He's looking healthier now, but I still haven't been able to find someone to repair his Symbio link with Rage. Clive's working on it, though. I worry more for her than him, what the quiet in her head must be like whilst she's out fighting our war.

When I go to bed, I think of Luca and my heart aches with a homesickness I've never experienced before. Without him I feel lost, but I know that he will come back to me and that we both had to choose our own paths. We couldn't stand in each other's shadows; we had to be our own people. We will be the stronger together for it.

I close my eyes, my hand over the patch on my uniform, and repeat the words in my head, "Whatever is rightly done, however humble, is noble," and I realise that I chose this path for the right reasons and that is honourable, despite the fact that I walked away. I don't believe it is cowardice, although Yve thought so, maybe even still thinks so. I believe I am doing the right thing. And, if I can help the children with me now, and others who have been taken by the GDO, then my war will be won. But theirs isn't over yet.

It doesn't matter how you resist oppression, so long as you resist it.

Acknowledgements

First, I want to thank the dream team, even though they are totally unaware they're part of a team: my superb editor Cressida Downing and my indispensable copyeditor Pam Firth. Both of you helped me to create *Rebellion,* and you've continued to be amazing with your work on *Resistance*.

A massive thank you to Monika MacFarlane for coming up with the incredible covers for this series.

A huge and heartfelt thanks to my Advance Reader Squad. You guys have been invaluable. ARS rules!

Kaitlin Throgmorton, also a member of ARS, went above and beyond helping me to pull this book together. Thank you for enjoying the creepy bits and for knowing when I was being just too damn "tight". You really helped me get to the finish line.

Michaela Pannese you goddam diamond — your unwavering faith keeps me going.

Natalie Flynn, you kept me sane (in the loosest sense of the term).

As always, my parents have been incredible. My mum was the first to read *Resistance* and give me the reassurance that it wasn't terrible. And dad for giving me the Helmuth von Molke quote and helping me fix that problematic first chapter. That thanks extends to my entire family; I just hope by now my nieces tell people I'm a writer and not an artist, like they mistakenly believed for years. I'm still not entirely sure why, but I went with it.

www.ingramcontent.com/pod-product-compliance
Lightning Source LLC
Chambersburg PA
CBHW031148120726
47905CB00006B/1865